Here Comes Charlie

by LANE PETERS

Illustrated by Gustave E. Nebel

SCHOLASTIC BOOK SERVICES
NEW YORK • TORONTO • LONDON • AUCKLAND • SYDNEY

Most of these stories appeared originally in *Calling All Girls,* published by Parents' Magazine Enterprises, Inc.

1st printing .... February 1970

Printed in the U.S.A.

CONTENTS

Charlie the Tree

Putting on a class play is hectic enough. With my cousin Charlie playing a tree, it's like trying to swim up Niagara Falls. I mean, take last week.

There I was, in the middle of my one important speech — the speech that, with any luck, might get me invited to join the Drama Club. As the wise servant girl, with my long hair tucked up inside a starched little cap, I was trying to persuade Princess Gloria that all was not lost. Even though we had barely escaped from her wicked uncle and had been chased into a dark and menacing forest; even though we were hungry and tired and frightened; even though a violent thunderstorm was about to break — was that any reason for us to be discouraged? Of course not!

"We'll be all right," I bravely assured the princess — or rather, my best friend, Mari Ann, who had the part. "We will be saved yet. Why, even Mother Nature is on our side. Look at yon friendly tree." Dramatically, I pointed to Charlie the tree, and waited. At this point, Charlie was supposed to spread his branches wide and beckon to us to come and take shelter. He spread his branches wide all right, and then hauled off and hit me with an acorn!

"Charlie Harris," I howled, forgetting about the princess and all her troubles, "that isn't in the script." Rubbing my cheek, I stormed over to where Charlie was leaning back against the blackboard and laughing. "You're supposed to be friendly, remember? And if you don't start being friendly, I'm going to slap you right in your bird's nest!"

Charlie, however, never takes my threats seriously. Laughing, he put down the branch he held.

"I'm just trying to liven things up, Cass," he explained. "That's the dullest speech I ever heard. Without my help, the audience is going to fall fast asleep on you."

"They will not," I began indignantly, but then stopped. What was the use? Bawling Charlie out only gets me laryngitis. He is the most aggravating boy in the world. What makes it worse our mothers felt we ought to be closer than most cousins just because we happened to be born on the same day. Like it or not, Charlie and I had been assigned to the same classes all through school. And the end was nowhere in sight!

Changing my tactics, I tried again. "Charlie," I sighed, pulling off my white cap and tossing it to the desk in sheer frustration, "you know I'm planning to be an actress some day. And how can I get experience if I don't get into the Drama Club? This is my big chance! Please cooperate."

"Is anything wrong, girls?" Miss Evans asked suddenly, stepping back into the room where we were rehearsing. "I thought I heard loud voices." She gave Charlie a thoughtful stare as she spoke, and he hastily picked up his branch and looked as innocent as a baby.

I hesitated. After all, Charlie *is* my cousin. Mari Ann, coming up beside me, gave my hand a squeeze as if to say the whole thing was up to me.

"Everything is coming along fine, Miss Evans," I said at last, and Charlie winked at me. "But do you think Charlie is right as a tree?" I went on, not daring to look at my redheaded cousin. "Don't you think he'd be better as one of the soldiers?"

Miss Evans raised one eyebrow. "Put a sword in Charlie's hands?" she asked, in mock horror. "Really, Cass, you know your cousin better than that. No, I think the play will be much better if we *root* Charlie in one spot."

"Yes, ma'am," I sighed, as Mari Ann giggled and even Charlie grinned. But I didn't think it was so funny. Making Charlie a tree probably was best for the play, but it certainly didn't do me much good. It was just my bad luck that I had to make my only important speech right under Charlie's branches. Even if he tried, I doubted if my energetic cousin *could* stand still for five or six minutes.

"Charlie's so fidgety," I complained to Mari Ann as we headed back to our Home Room after rehearsals. "He always has to be moving. Why, I bet that just when I have the audience in the palm of my hand, Charlie will bend down to tie his shoelaces. And how will that look?"

"Pretty funny," Mari Ann giggled again. "You hardly ever see a tree doing anything useful, Cass. They usually just stand around, and — " Her voice died away as I glared at her, and she gave me a sheepish grin. "I guess," she admitted, "it would sort of break the mood, though."

"It would *shatter* the mood," I told her sternly. There didn't seem to be much I could do about it, though. Trouble was, I reflected, tugging at my ear to help me think, Charlie is so chock-full of energy that some days his red hair and bright blue eyes seem to give out sparks. He couldn't play an overgrown vegetable any more than I could. Unless — it was then that I got this perfectly fiendish idea!

"Come on," I yelled, grabbing Mari Ann's arm. "I just figured out how to drain off some of Charlie's energy."

"Just don't borrow any of it," Mari Ann pleaded, as I pulled her back down the corridor. "I don't think I could stand it."

Back in the rehearsal room, we found Charlie busy playing a kind of golf. Using his branch as a club, he was trying to hit acorns into the waste basket and didn't look up as we came tearing in.

"Charlie," I gasped, skidding to a stop, "would you like to do me a tremendous favor?"

"No," Charlie answered, automatically. Taking careful aim, he swung his branch and sent a cup full of pencils flying off the teacher's desk. With a sigh, Charlie turned to me. "What kind of favor, Cass?"

When I get excited, I talk fast and right now the words tumbled out in a rush. "I promised Mrs. Jennings I'd sit with her little boy next Tuesday but I forgot it was the day of the play and now I'll be too busy, so could you — "

"Me?" Charlie broke in. "Baby-sit?" He pretended to be rocked back on his heels. "Have you blown your stack, Cass? Whatever made you think I'd do a goopy thing like that?"

"But, Charlie," I went on, forcing myself to slow down, "you're the only one in class who doesn't have any lines to rehearse. I can't ask anyone else."

"Nothing doing," Charlie shook his head emphatically and began picking up the pencils scattered over the floor. I stooped to help him, not licked yet.

"All right," I murmured, handing him a yellow crayon, "if you don't need the dollar an hour, I guess I can find someone else."

"Huh?" Charlie snapped to attention so quickly he almost dropped the pencils. "A dollar," he asked, his voice squeaking, "an hour?"

I nodded, and a broad grin spread all over Charlie's freckled face. As usual, he must have been stone-broke. Charlie's allowance is always being frittered away on luxuries like paying for broken windows. "Oh, boy," he exclaimed. "Lead me to it! Why didn't you tell me about this baby-sitting racket before, Cass?"

I didn't answer. I mean, why mention that most mothers don't pay such fantastic fees for an afternoon's work? Only the mother of a monster like Alfie Jennings has to offer that much, and at that, Mrs. Jennings has very few takers.

As a matter of fact, I had never promised to sit for Alfie this Tuesday or any other day. I knew better. But I was sure Mrs. Jennings would snap at the offer of a baby-sitter. And, of course, she did.

"Oh, Cassie," she breathed into the phone. "I haven't had a peaceful Tuesday in four and a half years. Thank you, dear, and thank that wonderful cousin of yours."

"Yes, ma'am," I murmured, glad that Mrs. Jennings couldn't see me blush. Oh, well, I told my uneasy conscience, it's for the good of the play. And Alfie and Charlie probably deserve each other.

I really was awfully busy the day of the play,

what with last-minute fittings and script changes. I didn't have time to think about Charlie until he failed to show up for dress rehearsal. Then I began to worry. After all, suppose something happened to Charlie. Aunt Carol would never forgive me. Remembering that one of Alfie's last baby-sitters had tripped on a toy fire truck and fallen down a flight of stairs, I chewed on my favorite fingernail and wondered if I'd gone too far.

But ten minutes before curtain time, Charlie showed up. Not a mark on him, either, I was relieved to see. "How did it go?" I asked curiously, as I helped him into his tree costume. "Did you and little Alfie get along all right?"

"Oh, sure. We played cowboy all day. I was the horse." Charlie yawned, and even his freckles looked tired. "Say, Cass," he burst out, "how do girls stand baby-sitting anyway?"

"Oh, we manage," I murmured, feeling guilty — but only a little. Anyone who's been a horse most of the day, I told myself contentedly, ought to be exhausted enough to stand still for a while. Though with Charlie you never could tell.

However, when the play started and I got caught up in the spirit of it, I gradually forgot about Charlie. I was busy trying to help Princess Gloria escape from her wicked uncle and when you're fighting off a squad of armed warriors you don't have time to think about trees. Toward the end of Act Two, Princess Gloria and I had to enter the Black Forest. Then I remembered Charlie in a hurry.

"Courage, Princess," I sang out, helping her along. "We will be safe from your uncle in this forest. These enormous trees will hide us from sight — " Then I got my first look at Charlie the Tree, and forgot all my lines. Charlie's branches were drooping almost to the ground. And his tree trunk looked as if it were made of rubber!

"C-courage, Princess," I repeated, feeling my own courage oozing out through my toes. "Everything will be f-fine." Edging over to Charlie as casually as possible, I bent down and pretended to pick up a leaf.

"Charlie," I whispered, into what I hoped was his ear. "Please stop playing games. There are five hundred people in the audience, so stand up and do your part right, will you?"

Anxiously, I waited. Then I heard — a gentle snore. Charlie, I realized with horror, was asleep!

For a few seconds, I just squatted there, too frozen to move. I had a wild impulse to kick Charlie awake, but realized in time it would look pretty silly. Anyway, it was all my fault. If only I hadn't wanted to tire Charlie out!

Then, Mari Ann, in her role as Princess Gloria,

was at my side. "Did you find anything, Marie?" she asked, in a queer, strained voice, and I remembered that I'd been bent down for quite some time. "Why, yes," I gulped straightening up and trying to think. "I, uh, found something for us to eat." I pretended to hand her something while I muttered under my breath, "Charlie's asleep. Get in front of him and help me hide him."

Jumping in front of that ridiculous drooping tree, I launched feverishly into my long inspirational speech. As I talked I could see, out of the corner of my eyes, the tree behind me beginning to sink lower and lower to the floor. Any second, I knew, Charlie was going to be stretched out flat on the stage. Desperately, I raised my voice in the hope that it might wake Charlie.

Finally, I finished and, heaving a sigh of relief, waited for the thunderstorm that was to end Act Two. It came — an ominous roll of drums. Then, the stage darkened, and the boy in charge of lightning started switching lights on and off very fast. At the same time, five or six kids began slamming brass cymbals together with all their might. The flashing lights and clanging cymbals made a pretty realistic storm. And, of course, it woke up Charlie.

"Fire!" he roared, in a voice that rose above the cymbals. "The place is on fire! Don't worry, Cass, I'll save you!" With that, a hand popped out of the tree trunk and grabbed mine. Before I could protest, I was being dragged around the stage by a yelling tree.

"Charlie, will you let go!" I screamed, as my cap fell off and my long hair came tumbling down. "You're in the school play, remember? You're playing a tree! Stop running!"

I got through to him at last. Of course, by that time we were off the stage and into the wings where the rest of the cast was standing around, giggling.

"My gosh, I forgot about the storm," Charlie groaned, in an agonized voice. "What a dope I am. Sorry, Cass, but I'll make it up to you. We'll go right back on stage and do it right."

"Oh, no, no," I moaned, digging my heels into the ground. It was no use; in a second I was being dragged right back in front of a howling audience.

"Charlie Harris," I told him, while waiting for the audience — and Princess Gloria — to stop laughing, "one of these days you are going to be sorry. For two cents, I would sell you for firewood!"

But by then the audience had begun to calm down. And, the play had to go on, no matter what. Even if my acting career was doomed, I could at least obey that famous rule. Smoothing back my tumbled hair with dignity, I marched back to Princess Gloria whose eyes were still filled with tears of laughter. "Everything will turn out fine," I told her, in a slightly breathless voice, "even Mother Nature is on our side. Look at yon friendly tree — "

I pointed a trembling finger at Charlie, who promptly spread his branches even wider and beckoned to us. Princess Gloria and I settled down under his branches, the thunderstorm broke out once more, and eventually the curtain rang down on the most gruesome Act Two in history.

Well, we got through the rest of the play somehow. I no longer cared much, but the audience loved us.

While I was still taking off my stage make-up, Norma Beasley, president of the Drama Club, came over and invited me to join.

"You mean you liked the play?" I asked incredulously.

"Well, not all of it," Norma admitted, sitting down beside me. "But the members and I just loved the way you did your two speeches. That note of desperation in your voice was so authentic!"

"It certainly was," I agreed, and all at once I was able to laugh for the first time. I felt so good, in fact, that I decided to forgive Charlie.

But it's the last time I'm getting on a stage with him!

The Phantom Burglar

WHEN my cousin Charlie decided to be a part-time detective, I knew he had flipped his redheaded lid. I mean, just because Charlie lives next door to a *real* detective — Mr. Mitchell, that is — he's hardly an authority on criminals. So Charlie couldn't possibly capture the Phantom Burglar. Or could he? Well, as a matter of fact . . .

But maybe I'd better start at the beginning, which was that grisly evening, three weeks ago, that I spent baby-sitting with the Mitchells' little boy, John. John, who is better known as J.M., the Juvenile Monster, sneaked up on me with his father's handcuffs and before I knew it, there I was — handcuffed to the Mitchells' radiator!

The whole thing got me so rattled that I admit I lost my head. Fortunately the telephone was within reach. With my free hand, I dialed Charlie — of all people — for help. "Please, Charlie," I wailed, when I'd explained what had happened, "you've just got to come next door and get me loose." "Right now?" Charlie wanted to know, as though I might prefer to spend a few more hours hooked to my favorite radiator. "Listen, I'm pretty busy. In fact, I'll be tied up for a while."

"Not as badly as I'll be," I pointed out, rattling the steel cuffs into the phone. "Charlie Harris, I really need you. These handcuffs aren't toys, you know, they're the real thing. And J.M. not only hid the keys somewhere in the house, but he's vanished himself. I haven't the foggiest notion where he's hiding and I don't know what I'll tell the Mitchells and — " I had to stop because Charlie was laughing so hard. That redheaded clown! Brushing the hair out of my eyes, I glared at the phone. When Charlie finally calmed down, he agreed to come over.

"I wanted to talk to you anyway, Cassie," he added. "I think I've figured out who the Phantom Burglar is. And if you're lucky, I'll let you help me catch him."

"Who me?" I yelped. But Charlie had already hung up, and there was nothing I could do. Honestly, if it weren't for those miserable handcuffs, I'd have raced for home and hidden under the bed. Help catch the Phantom Burglar indeed!

Not that he really was a phantom, of course. Leaning back and resting on my elbows, I tried to consider the matter calmly. The Phantom Burglar was just an ordinary thief who had broken into about fifteen homes in the past six months. The trouble was,

he hadn't exactly broken into them, he had just sort of *drifted* inside. None of the windows had been forced and none of the doors had been jimmied.

And there I was, alone in this house, with just fiendish J.M. for company! Beginning to shiver, I rolled the sleeves of my sweater down as far as they'd go and wished Charlie would hurry. When I finally heard his knock at the door, I found I was still in trouble — the front door was locked!

"Oh, no," I groaned, trying frantically to pull my hand out of the handcuffs. I couldn't, of course. But I did hear a scuffling noise behind the sofa and a faint muffled giggle. Taking a deep breath, I called out as pleasantly as I could, "J.M., dear, there's someone at the front door. Why don't you open it and see who it is?"

Nothing happened.

Gritting my teeth, I tried again. J.M. refused to crawl out from his hiding place, however. I was just resigning myself to spending the evening on the floor when I heard a crash from the bedroom.

"What's that?" I yelled, sitting up in alarm.

"A lamp," Charlie called back, gloomily. "I, uh, bent it when I crawled in through the window." And then he was clumping into the living room, followed by Barnaby, his big, droopy-eared basset hound.

For once, I was really glad to see Charlie's silly freckled face under that mop of bright red hair that always looked like an unmade bed. I wasn't so sure about Barnaby, though. The clumsy-looking hound was so delighted to see me sitting on the floor that he practically launched himself at me and began licking my nose with all his might.

"All right, Barnaby, take it easy," I sighed, trying to push the big dope off my lap. Then I squinted up at my cousin. "Why did you bring *him* along?"

"Why not?" Charlie asked, a wide grin on his freckled face as he squatted down on the floor beside me. "You know I'm training old Barnaby to be a police dog. I'll need his help if I ever run into the Phantom Burglar."

"Oh, yoicks!" I exclaimed. Barnaby was the kind of dog who panicked every morning when the alarm went off. I could just see him helping to capture a burglar! "Anyway, you shouldn't be messing around with such dangerous things," I scolded Charlie. "It's up to the *police* to go around looking for criminals."

"I know that. But Cass, there's a hundred-dollar reward for information about the Phantom Burglar." Charlie's voice was almost awed. "You realize that if I had all that money, I could finally get out of debt? Boy, I haven't seen my allowance for so long, I've almost forgotten what it looks like."

I giggled at that. Charlie is the only boy I know whose allowance is always tied up in I.O.U.'s.

"Anyway," Charlie went on, "it's safe enough. I was only kidding about catching the Phantom Burglar myself, Cass. I'll tell the police who he is and let them do it. I've got *some* brains!"

"That's a relief." I stretched my cramped legs out and wiggled into a more comfortable position. "Only how could you possibly know who the Phantom Burglar is?"

Charlie stopped fiddling with my handcuffs and scratched his freckled chin thoughtfully. "Well, the police always figured the thief had to be a locksmith of some kind. Mr. Mitchell told me the thief must have made up duplicate keys for the houses he was going to burgle. Trouble is, the police couldn't find the right locksmith."

"And you could?"

"I was just lucky," Charlie said modestly. "See, I

was reading this old magazine Dad was going to throw out and I spotted an ad for a fourteen carat, solid gold door key. It seems that people send in a regular door key and this man — Abe Henchley, his name is — makes up a duplicate key in solid gold for them. Since Mr. Henchley isn't a regular lock-smith, and he hasn't run the ad for over a year, I figured he must be the only key-maker in town the police haven't checked. And I was right!"

With new respect, I stared at my cousin. There was only one thing that bothered me. "You mean people are goopy enough to spend good money for a solid gold key? Just to open an old wood door? They'd have to be crazy!"

"They would not!" a small indignant voice broke in on me. "Lots of people have gold keys. We got a gold key!"

About six feet away, J.M. stood scowling at us, his round little face stormy. "Aunt Cora gave it to us."

"Sure she did," I said soothingly. "But, J.M., I'd much rather see the key to these handcuffs. Why don't you be a good boy and get that for me?"

It didn't do me any good though. Little J.M. has a one-track mind. "We do too have a gold key and I'll prove it to you," he flung at me. Then he raced out of the room, his slippers making no sound against the carpeted floor.

Charlie watched him go, and his freckled face was strangely excited. "Say, wouldn't it be something if the kid is right? All the people who were robbed had a gold key. I've been talking to them and I know. So if the Mitchells have one, maybe they're next on the Phantom Burglar's list."

"You don't have to sound so happy about it," I pointed out, making a face at him. "Anyway, I don't believe J.M. can tell a gold key from a brass one. He's just a baby."

But J.M. must have heard his parents talking about the key, because he was right; it did turn out to be gold. The key J.M. dropped triumphantly onto my lap had 14K stamped on it, right under the Mitchells' name. And it was even attached to a gleaming real-looking gold key ring!

Hardly able to believe my eyes, I turned the gold key over in my hands. It was then that a terrifying thought struck me. "It's Friday," I whispered, turning to Charlie. "All the burglaries took place on Fridays! Oh, Charlie, maybe you're right! Maybe we're going to be burgled tonight!"

Charlie's blue eyes widened, and he stared at me. But then he jumped to his feet. "I could be wrong, too. Just in case, though, J.M. and I had better booby-trap the windows so the Phantom Burglar can't sneak up on us. And, uh, Cass — " Charlie looked unhappily at my handcuffs — "maybe it wouldn't be a bad idea if you phoned the police."

"The p-p-police?" I stuttered, beginning to shake like a loose windowpane. But it was obviously the only sensible thing to do, and as soon as Charlie and J.M., followed by the big basset hound, headed for the bedrooms, I reached for the telephone with my free hand.

"Sergeant Grogan here," a harsh voice snapped, almost at once. "Can I help you?"

"Would you please send someone over to 348 Farrell Street," I asked, in a breathless rush, "because the Phantom Burglar is going to be here any minute. We just found a gold key!"

"Just a minute, you found a *what?*"

"A key," I repeated impatiently, "you know, a solid gold key attached to a gold key ring. With the Mitchells' name on it."

"Naturally," the harsh voice agreed. "The Mitchells would want their name on a solid gold key. Listen, young lady, if you have information about the Phantom Burglar, why don't you come downtown to headquarters?"

"Because I'm handcuffed to the radiator," I explained. And that reminded me, "Oh, and could you send someone down with skeleton keys or something? I'm getting sort of tired."

"I'm getting tired myself." For some reason, the sergeant sounded annoyed. "And just how did you get handcuffed to a radiator, may I ask?"

"Well, J.M. — that's the Juvenile Monster — sneaked up on me."

"So it was a monster, was it?" the sergeant roared,

startling me so that I dropped the receiver onto my lap. I didn't have to pick it up, though, I could hear him fine. "Listen, young lady, a police sergeant is not a person to try tricks on. Now, you just hang up quick before I decide to have a talk with your parents. Understand me?"

"Yes sir," I whispered, and, with a nerveless hand, put the phone gently back onto its cradle.

Oh well, I tried to console myself, maybe the Phantom Burglar wouldn't be here this week. Maybe he'd wait until next Friday when Mr. Mitchell would be home. "Mr. Mitchell," I gasped, feeling like an idiot. Of course! He was the one I should have phoned first. The only trouble was that, when I dialed the number the Mitchells' had left me, I could only get a busy signal. And I kept getting a busy signal for the next ten minutes or so. By that time, my dialing finger was practically paralyzed and I was just about purple with frustration.

Fortunately, my cousin came back into the living room just then. "Well, J.M. and I have the windows all booby-trapped," he announced, as he tramped over to my side, followed by his helpers. "The Phantom Burglar will hear such a crash if he opens a window that he's bound to get scared away." The two boys and Barnaby were covered with dirt and all three looked disgustingly cheerful to me.

"That's fine," I sighed, shaking my head at them. "But you forgot something, didn't you, fellows?"

Charlie wiped a grimy hand on his jeans and then settled down on the floor. "What did we forget, Cass?"

"You forgot that the Phantom Burglar doesn't come in through a window," I explained sweetly, "he — "

"Would you put down that telephone, young lady?" a man's voice behind us asked softly.

" — comes in through the front door." I finished in a kind of paralyzed whisper, while all the bones in my body began to slowly melt away with terror. A tall thin man was standing in the hallway. He was dressed all in dark gray — slacks, sweater, handkerchief around his face — and, in one hand, a steel gray gun!

"Now, kids, I don't want anyone to get nervous," the Phantom Burglar said in his soft voice. "If you'll all sit there quietly, nobody can possibly get hurt. Redhead, hold that mutt, will you?"

"S-sure," Charlie agreed, and grabbed Barnaby with one hand. With my free hand, I held J.M. tightly by my side. As for me, I *couldn't* move. In fact, I had the feeling I'd never be able to move a muscle again!

"Fine, fine. Now everybody just sit there." The gray-clad thief tucked the gun out of sight, pulled out a large gray sack from a pocket, and began to move silently around the room, opening drawers and tossing things into his case.

"Hey, I was right," Charlie whispered, into my ear, his blue eyes bright with excitement. "Listen, Cass, did you phone the police?"

"Yes, but I don't think they believed me." I whispered back, unhappily. All of a sudden, I didn't feel like being in the middle of a fight between *real* cops and robbers.

"That funny man is taking Mama's silver vase," J.M. suddenly shouted. "Make him stop that, Cassie."

"I can't, honey," I told the little boy, reaching across Charlie to pat him. "But don't worry, it's just a game. Your daddy will fix it when he comes home."

But that wouldn't be for hours. And the Phantom Burglar was coming back to us again, the gun once more in his hands.

"You," he said softly, waving the gun at me, "Suppose you come along and show me where the jewels are kept."

"I can't," I gasped, hardly able to speak. "I'm handcuffed to this radiator."

Above the gray handkerchief-mask, the thief's dark eyes narrowed menacingly. "Let's not have any games, sister," he snapped, bending over me. And suddenly, there was a tremendous crash from the bedroom.

Barnaby, who had been quietly watching, let out a howl of terror at the unexpected noise. Lumbering to his feet, he made a frantic rush for the front door, knocking the Phantom Burglar to the floor. The burglar's gun fell from his hand and Charlie kicked it under the sofa!

"You'll pay for that," the thief snarled, his voice no longer soft. The thief's eyes blazed furiously at us, but he didn't dare waste any more time. Still holding his case filled with stolen goods he ran to the front door, swung it open — and found himself face to face with Mr. Mitchell.

"What's going on here?" J.M.'s father demanded, pushing the thief back into the living room.

"He's stealing Mama's silver vase, Daddy," J.M. called out, jumping to his feet and running to his father. "Make him give it back."

"I certainly will," Mr. Mitchell said, in a grim voice. At that moment, an enormous policeman came thundering into the living room.

"Who in the miserable blue blazes put all that junk on the window sill?" the policeman demanded, in a familiar-sounding roar.

"You did believe me after all!" I exclaimed.

"I did not," the sergeant snapped. "I happened to pass Farrell Street on my way home and decided to take a look at the address you gave me. And I saw that guy sneaking in through the front door. Say, young lady, you *are* handcuffed to that radiator, aren't you?"

"I sure am." In all the excitement, I had almost forgotten. "Please, please unlock me."

While Mr. Mitchell held on to the Phantom Burglar Sergeant Grogan whipped out a huge key ring and set me free.

Then, I said to Mr. Mitchell, "I tried to phone you, but I kept getting a busy signal."

Mr. Mitchell smiled at me. "That's because I was trying to phone *you*, Cassie. I kept getting a busy signal, so I decided to come home and see what was going on."

Well, it turned out fine in the end. Charlie got his hundred dollars reward. Of course, by the time he paid Mr. Mitchell for the things that had gotten broken in the bedroom — and paid all the other people he owed — he was broke again.

As for me, the thing that's making me really shiver is remembering what J.M. said, just before he went to bed.

"Let's always have Cassie for a baby-sitter," he told his father sleepily. "She's fun."

"Okay, sport, I'll ask her again next time your mother and I go out," Mr. Mitchell said. . . . And I'm shivering because I may not have a good enough excuse to get out of it!

Trader Charlie

Nothing my cousin Charlie does can surprise me any more. At least that's what I keep telling myself. But I'll admit I got sort of a jolt last Saturday. I mean, as I skipped down the steps of the public library, I spotted Charlie coming up the street. He was pulling a wagon, his red head bent low and his shoulders hunched with effort. On the wagon — and I had to blink several times to make sure I wasn't imagining it — was an enormous moose head!

"Charlie," I gasped, as my cousin and his creaking wagon pulled up to me, "what in the world are you doing with a moose head?"

"Trying to trade it, of course," Charlie answered, as if that were a perfectly normal way to spend a warm spring morning. Letting go of the wagon handle, he pulled a handkerchief out of his jeans and ran it over his flushed, freckled face. "You wouldn't want to have it, would you?"

"Me?" Startled, I turned to stare at the moose head. The head — definitely on the moldy side and kind

of cross-eyed — stared back at me. "I don't think he exactly goes with my room," I told Charlie, in what was the understatement of the year. "In fact, he'd probably clash with the chintz draperies Mom just made me."

"A moose head doesn't fit in every place," Charlie agreed. "But I'll get rid of old Herman here yet. Well, so long, Cass." Charlie reached down for the handle again, but I grabbed his arm.

"Wait a minute, Charlie. You didn't tell me where you got that thing. Or why you're trying to trade him."

Charlie looked embarrassed. Scratching his red

head, he said, "It started when I had that accident with Mom's tea set. Did you hear about it?"

"The whole neighborhood heard about it, Charlie."

Last week, Aunt Carol had asked Charlie to polish some silver for her. My kooky cousin decided to invent a new silver polish for the occasion — and his polish had eaten so many holes into Aunt Carol's beautiful silver teapot it looked like a strainer!

"The folks were kind of upset," Charlie sighed. "Dad told me to get rid of my chemistry set, *fast*. So I traded it to Pete Colby for a catcher's mitt and that gave me an idea. Why not keep trading until I got something worth twenty dollars? Then I could buy poor Mom another silver teapot."

"That makes sense," I admitted. "But, there's just one thing wrong, Charlie. Who's going to give you anything for this moldy old head?"

"Mr. Ambruster, that's who. He happens to collect moose heads." Taking a deep breath, Charlie rubbed his hands together, then began pulling the heavy wagon again. Absently, I stepped into place beside him, and took hold of half the handle.

"You're kidding, aren't you, Charlie? Nobody *collects* moose heads."

"Why not?" My cousin grinned at me. "They make dandy hat racks. Anyway, Mr. Ambruster collects all sorts of things. If I can't trade Herman to him for something worth twenty dollars, I'll *eat* my hat."

"You're not wearing a hat," I retorted, stopping

short so suddenly the wagon banged into my legs. It had suddenly dawned on me who Mr. Ambruster was. "And maybe that's why your brains are curdling, Charlie. You know you can't do business with Mr. Ambruster. He's the most dishonest man in town. Why, he cheats everybody!"

"He's not going to cheat a smart trader like me," Charlie said, pushing out his freckled chin. "How could he? If I keep my wits about me and think before I act, what could go wrong?"

I opened my mouth to answer him. Everybody knows that, with Charlie around, everything that *can* go wrong *will* go wrong! Still, even I couldn't see how trading a moose head could lead to serious trouble. So I just shrugged and decided to see what would develop.

Charlie was right about one thing. Mr. Ambruster took an immediate liking to Herman. He was all smiles as he stroked Herman's moldly old head and said that he certainly did want him for his collection. "And I have just the thing for you, Charlie," he added, grinning all over his thin, narrow-eyed face. "Come out to the garage, kids. I want to show you something."

That something was a bed — the biggest and wackiest-looking bed I'd ever seen. It was at least eight feet long, was made of iron — all rusted, of course — and on its huge iron headboard was mounted an honest-to-goodness miniature cannon!

"It's an antique bed," Mr. Ambruster explained. "General Driscoll had it made especially for him right after the Civil War. The general was close to seven feet tall, you see, and naturally he needed an oversized bed."

"Naturally," Charlie agreed, staring with awe at the giant bed. He seemed fascinated by the cannon, though how anyone could sleep under a thing like that was more than I could see. "It's quite a bed all right, Mr. Ambruster, but I'm not sure I could trade it to anyone."

"Why, of course you could," Mr. Armbruster said, grinning even more widely.

I began to get very nervous. "Charlie," I whispered, pulling at my cousin's sleeve, "the bed's all rusty. And I never heard of any General Driscoll."

But Charlie just shook my hand off. He never can resist anything that's twice as big as it ought to be. "If I thought anyone wanted a bed like that — "

"Why, Mr. Landers, the antique dealer, wants the bed, my boy. Just the other afternoon, Mr. Landers offered me twenty dollars for it. And sight unseen, too. But I've been so busy lately — "

"Twenty dollars!" Charlie burst out. "Hey, that's great. That's just what I need."

"Charlie," I moaned, shaking my head so hard it practically rattled. "Wait a minute."

But it wasn't any use. "I'll take the bed, Mr. Ambruster. And thanks a lot."

"Fine, fine. A wise decision." Mr. Ambruster's long narrow face looked an awful lot like the moose head, I thought glumly, as he turned to lead us back to the house. We were halfway down the driveway when the man paused. "Oh, by the way — "

My heart sank all the way down to my scuffed brown loafers. Here it came!

"You may have noticed that the iron bed is unusually large. It doesn't fit into Mr. Landers' pick-up truck and it certainly doesn't fit into my station wagon. Only the Comet Moving Company can handle furniture this big and, by odd coincidence, they asked twenty dollars to transport the bed for me."

"They asked *what!*" Charlie's freckled face was suddenly pale with anger. He ran his hand through his red hair until it stood up in spikes. "But that's not fair. You should have told me — ."

"That would have been foolish of me, wouldn't it? But don't worry," Mr. Ambruster smiled cheerfully at Charlie, "a bright boy like you should be able to think of a less expensive way to move that bed out of here. Now if you'll excuse me."

As Mr. Ambruster scurried away, Charlie sank down onto the edge of the giant bed. "Oh, that crook," he groaned.

"You're a smart trader all right," I sighed, reaching down to take a pebble out of my shoe.

Charlie scowled. "Listen, Cass, I'll get that bed

over to Mr. Landers' antique store, if I have to *push* it all the way."

"Push this iron monstrosity half a mile or more? Mr. Landers' store is on Callavan Street, you know."

Charlie turned to study the huge bed. "Maybe I could mount wheels on it," he said thoughtfully, "Maybe even put on a motor."

"Motorize a *bed?*" Appalled, I stared at my cousin.

"Why not?" Charlie's blue eyes got that faraway look that always made me wish I was far, far away myself. "I motorized my bicycle, didn't I? That means I have at least one motor I could borrow and Dad's old power lawn mower is still in our garage. If its motor still works, both motors together ought to give us all the power we need."

"What do you mean, *us?*" I yelped. "I'm not going to help you push any hotrod bed any where, any time. Not in a thousand years — not in a million years — not ever, understand?"

Naturally, next morning I was back at Mr. Ambruster's garage. Mari Ann was with me. I had told her all about the bed and the two of us just had to see if Charlie really could motorize it.

And apparently he could. At least, the bed was mounted on wheels and had some sort of motor strapped to each side. Ropes were everywhere, long ones, short ones, red ones, black ones, white ones —

35

"Hi," Charlie greeted Mari Ann and me, not looking at all surprised to see us. "Listen, will you girls hold on to Barnaby's leash? He keeps getting tangled up with the ropes."

Mari Ann took hold of Barnaby's leash, and the big dog licked her hand affectionately. "Why do you need so many ropes, Charlie?" she asked my cousin.

"Well, this rope here starts the motors," Charlie explained, pointing to the rope with the wrench he was holding. "And these two steer — but not too well, so I figure we better not start the motors till we get the bed away from the house. It might be safer."

"It might be safest if we set fire to the whole thing," I suggested. Charlie ignored me, however. He spent another few minutes fiddling with nuts and bolts and things. Then we got behind the silly contraption and pushed it down the driveway and out onto the sidewalk. Barnaby trotted along at out heels, occasionally racing forward to sniff suspiciously at a dangling rope or to bark at the wheels.

"Charlie," I breathed, straightening up and wiping my forehead with the sleeve of my sweater. "Are you sure those motors will make this thing any easier to push? Because we've only gone a couple of feet and I'm pooped."

"Don't worry. The first few blocks are mostly downhill, anyway and — hey, grab the bed!" The iron monstrosity was starting to roll. I made a grab for one of the dangling ropes which proved to be an awful mistake. The motors suddenly sprang into noisy life and the bed put on a burst of speed!

"Great galloping galoshes," Charlie yelled. Sprinting after the bed, he jumped onto it and reached for the steering ropes. Barnaby leaped onto the bed, too, barking with delight. He loves to go riding.

"Charlie, get that poor dog off," Mari Ann ordered, her round face flushed with concern. "It's dangerous!" She grabbed one of the bed posts and hung on. Thinking, for some insane reason, that our weight might slow the monster down, I grabbed for the other bed post and we were off, racing down Myrtle Street and picking up speed every second!

"Charlie, can't you stop this thing?" I gasped, managing to swing myself onto the rusty, sagging bed springs. "Put on the brakes."

"Don't have any," Charlie called over his shoulder, a steering rope around each wrist. "I never figured we'd be going this fast. Listen, Mari Ann, release that orange rope, will you? That ought to stop the motors."

"I can't," Mari Ann wailed. "Barnaby has it in his mouth!"

"Oh, that's just great! Well, if we all hang on real tight — uh — " As we neared the corner, suddenly a woman wheeling a baby carriage came out of her house. Charlie pulled at one of the steering ropes with all his might. The bed veered sharply to the right, off the sidewalk and out onto the street at a crazy angle.

"Straighten out the wheels, Charlie," I yelled. "We have to go straight or we'll wind up on Main Street and — oh, *yoicks!*"

Because that's where we were, heading straight down the busiest street in town. Of course, it was Sunday and traffic wasn't as bad as it might have been. But there were enough cars to make me close my eyes tight, hold onto the bed post for dear life, and *pray!*

All around me, horns were blaring, people were screaming, whistles were blowing —

Whistles? Horrified, I opened my eyes. "It's a policeman, Charlie. He wants you to pull over."

"Don't I wish I could," Charlie sighed. "Say, you know, we've got real good drivers in this town. Look at that big red car dodge out of our way. And that bus — "

"Bus?" Moaning, I closed my eyes and prayed again.

"The policeman is running after us," Mari Ann called out.

"Never mind him, what about the bus?"

"Missed us by a good six inches. Don't worry about a thing" — the bed suddenly shot to one side, knocking me flat onto Barnaby — "here's Callavan Street, and it's uphill. That should slow us."

And it did, finally. Just about the time that the

red-faced traffic policeman managed to catch up with us.

He was too out of breath to talk, at first. Then he got out one sentence. "The entire lot of you are under arrest."

Weakly, the three of us tottered off the iron bed. "You don't really have to arrest us, do you?" Charlie asked. "It was all an accident. See, my dog had the rope in his mouth and — "

The policeman let out a roar of rage. "Don't tell me the dog was driving that heap, sonny. I saw you up front steering it. Now, I'm charging you with reckless driving, driving without a license, driving without proper headlights, driving up a one-way street, disturbing the peace — " Just then, the iron bed collapsed, scattered rusty metal springs all over the place. "And littering the sidewalk."

The policeman went on and on. After a while, I stopped listening. Trying to straighten out my wind-blown hair with one shaking hand, I just wondered if our families had enough money to pay the various fines we seemed to be accumulating.

It turned out that they did. Or at least Aunt Carol and Uncle Ben did, since only Charlie was fined.

The judge, after listening to our story, first shook his head and said he didn't really believe the whole thing. "Mass hallucination," he muttered. "There *couldn't* have been a bed hurtling down Main Street with three children and a dog on it." After studying the photograph in the afternoon paper, he sighed and added, "But you were driving some sort of contraption, young man. Since you've told me how sorry you are and since nobody was hurt, I'm fining you only fifty dollars. If I ever see you in my court again, you'll be extremely sorry."

Charlie already was about as sorry as I'd ever seen him. Along with everything else, he was now about seventy dollars in debt to his parents, a record even for him.

"If it would make you feel any better," I told him later, "I'll get you another chemistry set and you can start trading all over again."

Charlie rubbed his red head as if it were aching. "Would you mind not mentioning the word 'trading' ever again? I don't even want to think about this whole miserable — " But just then the telephone rang. And it was Mr. Landers, the antique dealer.

"Can I speak to the driver of the bed?" he asked pleasantly. Handing the receiver to Charlie, I put my head close to his so I could listen in, too.

"Well, Charlie, I picked up the pieces of your bed to see if anything could be salvaged," Mr. Landers began. "And you'll never guess what I found stuffed deep into that old cannon."

"A cannon ball?" Charlie asked hopefully.

"Of course not. I found General Driscoll's *diary*, the one his family could never find. It seems General Driscoll used to write his diary in bed — "

"And then stuffed it into the cannon's muzzle?" I broke in excitedly.

"Apparently. At the time of the general's death, no one thought to look for it there. And so it's been missing for a good many years," Mr. Landers told us.

"And you thought there wasn't any General Driscoll," Charlie whispered to me, making a face, and then took a deep breath and turned back to the telephone. "Is the diary worth anything, Mr. Landers?"

"That's hard to say, Charlie. The Civil War Society in town probably would like to have it and the general's family, too. I could try selling it for you and collect a commission. Or, I could buy it outright from you, for seventy-five dollars."

"I'll take it," Charlie shouted into the phone and then let out a war whoop that brought my mom running from the kitchen to see who was being scalped.

Actually, Mr. Landers wound up giving Charlie fifty dollars, an antique silver teapot Aunt Carol had always wanted, and the small iron cannon as a souvenir of our wild bed ride. So it all turned out pretty well in the end *except* — Charlie says he's going to take the cannon and see if he can trade his way up to a new bicycle. I hope the town and I can survive!

Charlie Flies a Kite

A PHONE CALL from my cousin Charlie always means trouble. That's because Charlie doesn't like to waste the telephone and he only uses it when he has a project in mind — some simple little idea that's bound to end in utter disaster. Like last Tuesday.

"Cassie," Charlie began, as soon as I'd picked up the receiver, "would you please come over and help me fly my kite?"

"Never in a million years," I answered automatically, then blinked and stared at the phone, wondering if I'd heard right. As far as I knew, Charlie had given up kites years ago. "Did you say you had a kite?" I asked.

"This is for a science project, Cass. You know, like Benjamin Franklin and his kite?"

"You mean you're planning to get us electrocuted?" I shrieked.

Charlie gave a snort of exasperation. "Will you stop being so silly, Cass, and come on over? All I'm asking you to do is help me fly an innocent little kite so I can win this term's Science Award. What could possibly go wrong?"

"Practically anything," I retorted. Settling down cross-legged on the floor, I tugged thoughtfully at my hair and tried to make sense out of the conversation. Naturally, I knew my kooky redheaded cousin always did things the hard way. Still, how could he expect a kite to help him win a science award? Though I tried hard to fight it, curiosity began to get the better of me.

"Well, maybe I could come over for a while," I said at last, leaning back against the telephone stand. But then I remembered the letter I had to mail.

All the girls in my class had formed a Ricky Ryder fan club. I was the only one, though, who hadn't gotten the sweater — you know, the bright red one with Ricky's name embroidered on the collar. The way money sort of slithers through my fingers, it had taken me three months — baby-sitting like mad whenever I had the chance — to save the ten dollars the sweater cost. But now I finally had it, and I knew I'd better get it into the mail fast.

"I can't stay long, Charlie," I warned him, explaining about the money I had to mail. "I've got to buy a stamp before the post office closes."

"Don't worry, Cass," my big-hearted cousin said, "if you do a good job helping me, I'll *give* you a stamp."

"Boy, what a sport!" I hung up. Then, knowing

how exhausting helping Charlie can be, I changed into my oldest shorts and an orange sweater that had faded in spots.

Just the same, scuffing on my way to Charlie's house, I had a feeling I was making a mistake. Because, when you stop to think about it, why did Charlie need my help at all? He's a lot bigger now than he was in the second grade and could certainly handle the biggest kite without me. And no matter what else is wrong with that boy, I have to admit that he's the top science student in school. In fact, our science teacher says he expects Charlie to be the first man on Mars some day; with or without a space ship. So it wasn't my scientific help Charlie needed.

It was a mystery, all right. And when I reached the house and headed down to the basement where Charlie does most of his work, the sight of that kite didn't explain a thing. Because Charlie's kite, believe me, was the wackiest thing I've seen in my life. It was practically shapeless, about six feet long and a brilliant plaid!

"Charlie Harris," I gasped, dropping my letter to Ricky Ryder on the work table, "have your brains finally curdled? That isn't a kite; it's a color-blind nightmare. Why, I'll bet you won't even get it off the ground!"

"Funny, that's what they said to the Wright Brothers." Charlie grinned at me. He was wearing his "inventing pants," a pair of faded and patched jeans that Aunt Carol has been trying to throw out for a year now. "I can't help the color, Cassie. I had to make the kite out of rubber, and this old plaid raincoat was the only thing I could find."

"A rubber kite," I murmured, still unable to take my eyes off the wacky-looking contraption. "A plaid rubber kite!"

"Naturally." Charlie ran a hand over his spiky hair. "And it's great! Matter of fact, I'm planning to fly it clear across the Atlantic Ocean."

"Aren't you afraid you'll get your feet wet?"

Feebly, I sank down onto the bench next to Charlie's worktable, convinced that this time my cousin really had flipped. Maybe, I thought, chewing on my knuckle, I ought to call Aunt Carol.

But Charlie sounded no daffier than usual. "Stop being silly, will you, Cass? The whole thing is very scientific. Actually, I'm not even flying a kite. What I'm doing is measuring air currents. Here's how it works — "

But the door to the back yard crashed open just then, and young John Mitchell came racing into the basement. "Hi," he yelled, his round smudged face beaming. "Let's play ball, Charlie!" And he threw a baseball at Charlie's head.

Catching the ball with one hand, Charlie sighed. "Hello, J.M. Are you through playing in our yard?"

I blinked at that as Charlie's yard is off-limits to J.M. This afternoon, though, he looked completely at home. Watching the way he settled down to examine Charlie's tool box, I suddenly felt the first prickling of suspicion.

"How come you're being so nice to J.M. today, Charlie?" I asked, narrowing my eyes. "You aren't by any chance supposed to be baby-sitting with him, are you?"

"Who me?" But Charlie gulped, and ran his hand guiltily over his red hair. "Well, I did sort of break the Mitchells' picture window, Cass," he admitted, not looking at me. "The only way I can pay them is by looking after the Juvenile Monster — the kid, I mean. And, honest, Cass, I just have to get this kite finished today, and — "

"Nothing doing," I broke in, snatching up my letter. I finally knew why Charlie had invited me over, and I wanted no part of it. I only baby-sit with the Juvenile Monster in dire emergencies, and, besides, nothing makes me madder than being tricked. "I should have known you really didn't want my help on a science project, Charlie. Especially when I saw that kooky-looking kite."

"But I wasn't kidding, Cass," Charlie protested, grabbing my arm. "I really am going to measure air currents with that kite. Listen," and he began to talk very fast the way he always does when he's in trouble. "See, when I release the kite, I attach my name and address to it and ask the finder to write and tell me where the kite landed. That way, I've got an idea of the directions of the air currents. With any luck, I can even figure out their speed. Do you follow me?"

"I'm trying to lose you, Charlie," I snapped, still trying to pull my arm free. Charlie held on, though, his blue eyes gleaming with excitement, and continued giving a long and involved lecture on measuring air currents. Apparently, he was the first person who'd ever thought of using kites. After a while, I just gave in, worn out by all that wind. I mean, who was I to stand in the way of scientific progress?

"All right, all right," I told him. "I'll look after J.M. till you finish that kite. But I'll bet Madame Curie never started like this."

Which explains why, five minutes later, I was outside and wasting a perfectly beautiful blue-sky spring afternoon by playing catch with the Juvenile Monster. To make things worse, J.M. was an absolutely wild ball-thrower. Half the time, he even missed the house behind us and I had to keep racing out into the street to hunt for the ball. Honestly, the whole thing was pretty depressing.

I was out on the sidewalk on my hands and knees for about the fortieth time when Mari Ann came by. "Cassie Quinn," Mari Ann asked, stopping short, "whatever are you doing down there?"

Settling back on my heels, I tossed the hair out of my eyes and blinked up at her. "Helping Charlie measure air currents, of course," I told Mari Ann with dignity. "What does it look like I'm doing? And don't bother to answer." As usual, Mari Ann was wearing a dazzling clean starched white blouse and a brilliant plaid skirt. Looking at my own grimy hands made me feel grubby as a pup in a sandbox. Before I could clean myself up a little, though, Charlie was shouting over the fence at us.

"Hey, Cassie, hey, Mari Ann," he yelled, his red hair sticking straight up with excitement, "I've got it finished. Come on and see it. The kite, that is," he added for Mari Ann's benefit.

Mari Ann's round face was blank. "A kite?" she asked in a mystified voice as we headed back to the yard.

Charlie heard her. "Wait till you see it. It's immense. I left it tied to the basement door, and — hey!" Charlie turned and his blue eyes widened. We could see J.M. busily playing with the kite's string. Charlie let out a roar. "John, no! Don't touch that kite! Get away from it quick!"

The smudge-faced little boy hated to be told what to do, though. At Charlie's order, J.M. defiantly yanked the string free and even as Charlie raced to reach him, the kite, with J.M. still holding on to it, began to rise up off the ground!

"Catch him," I gasped, so excited I didn't even stop to wonder how the whole thing was possible. I mean, I could see the huge plaid kite, easily twice

as tall as J.M., soaring up into the sky and pulling
the little boy with it.

The three of us all raced to get to J.M. In the
excitement, however, Charlie tripped and Mari Ann
and I stumbled over him. By the time we got ourselves unscrambled, we were too late. J.M. had flown
up even out of Charlie's reach.

Fortunately, the giant kite had stopped rising, at
least for the time being. It was brushing up against
the top branches of the yard's oak tree and seemed
to be tangled.

"J.M.," Charlie called, getting in position under
the boy, with his arms out wide, "let go of the string.
Don't be afraid because I'll catch you."

But J.M. just smiled down at us. "Look," he yelled, gleefully, "I'm flying a great big kite."

"The kite is flying *you*, you little dope," Charlie snapped, still holding his arms out. "Now stop fooling around and let go of that string!"

"I won't," J.M. answered, sticking his tongue out at Charlie. For good measure, he clutched at the string with both chubby hands and began to bounce up and down. The kite pulled free of the top branches and began to rise again.

Beside me, Mari Ann moaned. I could practically see J.M. being dragged halfway across the ocean by that huge kite and for a second, I stood there, paralyzed with fright.

But then, in a last desperate effort, I screamed out, "J.M., catch the ball!" And I threw it upward as hard as I could.

J.M. reached out both hands for the ball the way he always did, and he promptly fell straight down in the general direction of Charlie's head.

Well, it was a mixed-up tangle for a while. When Mari Ann and I got the boys straightened out, J.M. turned out to be fine, which was certainly a relief. Charlie had the beginnings of a black eye, though.

"A scientist has to expect a few accidents," Charlie sighed, and stared sadly up at the sky with his good eye. The kite, which looked like a giant plaid fish, was turning somersaults in the air. It was an eerie sight, and Mari Ann said it made her seasick.

"Anybody who could design a wacky-looking thing like that," she told Charlie, with a sniff, "has no business looking after an innocent little child. I'm going to take him right home and advise his mother to keep him away from you."

"Best news I've heard all day," Charlie said, brightening. We were both silent as Mari Ann marched J.M. out of the yard. Then we went back into the basement.

"Well, I guess this is one science award you're not going to win," I told Charlie. Dipping my handkerchief in cold water, I handed it to him and waited while he cleaned J.M.'s footprints off his face. "By the way, didn't it seem strange that the kite managed to lift J.M. off the ground. I mean, I know he's only a little kid, but — "

"That's easy to figure out. It was a balloon kite. It was full of helium," Charlie explained. He crumpled my grimy handkerchief up into a ball and held it to his eye. "How else did you think a kite could fly all the way across the Atlantic?"

Actually, I hadn't thought about it at all. I mean, what do I know about kites? "Let's forget the whole thing, Charlie. I'm sorry about the science award, though."

"Oh, I still have a chance of getting my kite back. Before it was even finished, I tied my letter of explanation to it. That means I can still measure the air currents around here. Say, did I tell you how the scheme works?"

"You sure did," I put in hastily, before he could begin that lecture again. "Just one thing I don't understand. How could you have attached your letter of explanation to the kite when the letter is right there by the glue pot?"

"It can't be," Charlie protested, dropping the handkerchief from his eye. He reached for his letter. "I know I attached an envelope to that kite. I remember it distinctly. It was — uh, oh!"

"My letter!" I yelped, jumping to my feet. "You took my letter with the ten dollars I slaved to earn and sent it flying off into *nowhere!* Maybe all the way to Europe?"

"It was an accident," Charlie groaned. "I told you a scientist has to expect a few accidents, didn't I?"

"Well, here's another accident you can add to your collection," I snarled, reaching for the glue pot. But of course, I didn't throw the pot at Charlie. There are some things a girl can't do, much as she'd like to. So, I just stormed around the basement awhile, telling Charlie what I thought about him and his miserable kite. And then I went home, vowing that I'd never, never go near that redheaded cousin of mine until we were both ninety years old.

I meant it too. However, the very next morning, there was a phone call from the *Daily Courier*, asking to speak to Miss Cassie Quinn.

"Miss Quinn," a stern voice demanded, when I picked up the receiver, "are you the young lady who launched the plaid contraption that's been terrifying the whole town?"

"M-m-me?" I stammered, falling into the armchair next to the phone. "You mean, Charlie's kite has been scaring people?"

"Is that thing a kite?" The man's voice sounded stunned. "Thought it was a plaid zeppelin, myself. Well, anyway, Miss Quinn, your kite was shot down an hour ago, and we'd like to get the story on it. Is it supposed to be a method of beating the post office out of an airmail stamp? Because if it is — "

"It's supposed to be measuring air currents," I explained as quickly as I could. If there was one thing I didn't want, it was to have the F.B.I. think I was tampering with the mails. "My cousin Charlie can tell you about that. Only, why was the kite shot down?"

"Oh, somebody started a rumor that a plaid flying saucer was over town. It did look pretty spooky, at that. Instead of little plaid men, though, all we found was your letter. Incidentally, Miss, what does a Ricky Ryder sweater have to do with measuring air currents?"

"It's a very long story," I sighed, and advised him to take the whole matter up with Charlie. The reporter took Charlie's name and address, then promised I'd hear from him again.

And I certainly did. The whole story (except for the part about J.M.'s flight, fortunately) was splashed over the front page that very afternoon. I would have died out of sheer embarrassment, except that Ricky Ryder himself phoned to thank me for the publicity I'd gotten him.

"Wish all my fans were as original as you are, Cassie," he said, while I sat in a kind of daze, listening. "Imagine mailing a letter to me by kite. Keep up the good work, honey. And by the way, I'm sending you one of my own sweaters absolutely free!"

"Ulp," I answered brightly. I think maybe I fainted.

If Charlie wants more help in trying for that science award, though, I've got my answer ready. I plan to tell Charlie to go fly a kite!

Charlie Does It Again

IF THERE'S one thing I've learned it's that asking my cousin Charlie for help is like asking for instant disaster. But when I tried to explain this to Norma Beasley, the president of our Drama Club, she just snorted. "Don't be silly, Cass. After all, Charlie has a talking crow — even if it hasn't learned how, yet. Charlie could teach him. You said Charlie has a way with birds and animals and things."

"But Oswald couldn't learn in time for the play!" I exclaimed. "That's only a few days!"

"It's bad enough we can't get a real parrot for our play," Norma went right on as though she hadn't heard me. "But if I have to walk around the stage with a crow on my shoulder, the least he can do is talk to me. So, call your cousin!"

It was an order, delivered in the voice Norma uses to get our club to come to order. Since it's a very difficult voice to argue with, I sighed and gave in. Let Norma learn the hard way!

Over the telephone, I explained the Drama Club's

predicament to Charlie. We were planning to put on a pirate play as our contribution to the "Get the School a Library" campaign. Norma was playing Long Lucy Silver, a lady pirate, and the part called for her to carry a parrot — a parrot who kept saying, "Avast there, you lubbers."

"What does that mean?" Charlie, who was naturally nosy, asked.

"How should I know? But it adds a touch of realism to the play. That's what Mrs. Granger, our director, keeps telling us. She is a firm believer in realism. Anyhow, we can't get a real parrot, so we want to use Oswald instead. He's *supposed* to be a talking crow. You could teach him even if he hasn't let out a peep so far."

"Say, I have a new idea," Charlie said. "I bet if I crossed Oswald with a homing pigeon, I'd get a kind of carrier crow who could deliver — "

"Charlie," I yelped, pulling at my hair in frustration, "will you pay attention! The play opens in less than a week!"

"That doesn't give us much time," Charlie agreed, sounding disgustingly cheerful. "But you're in real luck, Cass. I've just invented a gizmo that will solve all your troubles."

Well, naturally — knowing Charlie and his inventions — I turned pale and considered withdrawing from the play altogether. Let it blow up without me! Unfortunately, I did have the second lead and it *was* for the benefit of the school library. "Okay, Charlie, bring the gizmo over to the school auditorium tomorrow around three. But I have a feeling I'm not going to like it."

And I didn't. Charlie's gizmo turned out to be a kind of miniature transistor radio, small enough to be strapped around Oswald.

"See, it's perfectly simple," Charlie said briskly. "I just have to tie the radio to Oswald. Then I can stand backstage, talk into this little microphone and it will sound as if Oswald is talking."

"Why, what a wonderful idea," Norma gasped, staring at my redheaded cousin with wide, admiring eyes. "And we won't have to worry about Oswald forgetting his cues. Don't you think Charlie is a genius, Cass?"

I just gulped. All the horrible things that could happen with my kooky cousin talking into a microphone before a large audience flashed before my eyes and I was too stunned to say a word. When I finally opened my mouth, it was too late. Charlie had already headed for Oswald to attach what he called his "Flyie-Talkie."

And, unfortunately, the contraption worked. From the audience, it did seem as if Oswald were talking. The voice sounded like Charlie's of course, but few people would notice that. So I knew that we were stuck with both Charlie and his radio.

"I don't know why you keep expecting the worst,"

Norma scolded me, the night after our dress rehearsal. The other kids had gone home. We had stayed behind, in the small dressing room back of the school auditorium, and were busy putting red and yellow feathers onto Oswald. This was partly to make him look more like a parrot and partly to hide the tiny radio. "It's been a whole week, and the radio's worked like a charm every time."

"Just wait," I prophesied. Norma and I hadn't bothered getting out of our costumes. She was dressed as a pirate, a scarf covering her hair and a black patch over one eye. Since I was playing an Indian, I had on a brown fringed leather jacket, a beaded belt, and moccasins. "Something terrible will happen. It always does."

"Oh, pooh." Norma waved a red feather at me. "If you want to worry, Cass, worry about the tickets we haven't sold yet. Why, except for our relatives, there may be no one at all in the audience tomorrow!"

"We'll sell some tickets at the door," I reminded her, mostly to cheer her up. Privately, I had a feeling our play wasn't going to help the school library campaign much. And it seemed a shame after the way all of us, including Oswald, had worked. But there wasn't much we could do about it.

Just then, there was a knock at the door and Mrs. Granger, our director, came in. She had a dignified, gray-haired lady with her. "Girls, this is Mrs. Stanpoole, the guest of honor at the faculty dinner tonight. I know you've been worried about the ticket sales, so I thought I'd tell you. Mrs. Stanpoole is so interested in seeing that we get our school library she's agreed to buy every unsold ticket!"

"Why, that's wonderful!" We jumped up to thank Mrs. Stanpoole, forgetting all about our dirty sticky hands. But Mrs. Stanpoole turned out to be a darling. She didn't mind the stickiness, and was so interested in our plan to turn Oswald into a parrot that she decided to stay and talk to us while Mrs. Granger attended to some errands in the building.

We had just finished giving Mrs. Stanpoole the

whole plot of our pirate play when there was another knock on the door. This time it was Charlie and he had his dog Barnaby with him.

"Oh, Charlie, don't bring Barnaby in here," I protested, with a sidelong look at Mrs. Stanpoole. It was a small room, and not everyone likes dogs.

"That's all right, Cass," Mrs. Stanpoole murmured, but her face did seem a little pale. Barnaby is an enormous hound, though perfectly gentle. "I'm sure he's a very well-behaved animal."

"Well, as a matter of fact," I began — because Barnaby is sort of nervous and I like to be honest — I didn't get a chance to finish, because Barnaby spotted Oswald just then and let out a howl.

The howl sounded twice as loud as usual in the small dressing room. With a squawk of terror, Oswald flew off the dressing table, soared over Barnaby's head, and made for the door. Charlie slammed it in the nick of time but that didn't stop Oswald. Cawing wildly, he circled Barnaby's head. Barnaby howled louder than ever, and for a few seconds, the scene in the dressing room was a pretty wild one, what with Barnaby howling, Oswald squawking, and Norma, Charlie, and me trying to catch Oswald.

But finally, Oswald spotted the open window and flew out like an arrow. Charlie quieted his dog down, and it was suddenly strangely still in the dressing room.

"Well," Norma said after a few seconds, "let's not

just stand here. We've got to go out and find Oswald."

"If we can," I sighed. "Mrs. Stanpoole, I'm terribly sorry about the fuss, but — Mrs. Stanpoole?" To my astonishment, the dignified, gray-haired lady was nowhere in sight.

"Here I am, Cassandra," Mrs. Stanpoole called out. "I stepped into the closet to get out of the confusion. But I'm afraid that the door locked on me. I think I saw the key on the dressing table. Would you please — ?"

"Just a minute, Mrs. Stanpoole," I called back. I hurried to the table. But the key was not there. Norma and Charlie came over to help me search. We got down on our knees, spurred on by the thought of poor Mrs. Stanpoole locked in the coat room. After a frantic few minutes of search, though, we had to admit it. The key simply wasn't in the room.

"But I saw it on the table myself," Norma whispered. "It couldn't have just flown away — oh!"

The thought struck us all at the same instant. Oswald! Norma turned paper white and stared fearfully at the locked closet. "Oh, Cass, we're in terrible trouble! Mrs. Stanpoole is a wonderful person, but even she is going to be furious about this. If she's locked up for much longer, she'll probably wash her hands of the whole school library campaign!"

"Children, is anything wrong?" Mrs. Stanpoole's voice, muffled but anxious, came through the door.

"Whatever is taking so long? Why aren't you unlocking the closet?"

We looked at each other. Then Norma and I both turned to Charlie. He took a deep breath and confessed, "We can't seem to find the key, Mrs. Stanpoole. But don't worry. Just sit tight, and we'll get the janitor."

"Charlie, he's gone home," Norma whispered. "It's after hours."

"Then we'll find Oswald," Charlie whispered back. "Don't worry. Listen, Norma, you see if you can hunt up the janitor. Maybe you can find out his home address. Cass, you go out and see if you can spot Oswald. Here, take these peanuts. Oswald loves them."

Norma and I took off on the run. It wasn't until I was out in the street that it occurred to me I had no idea of what Charlie was going to do. It was too late to go back now, though.

"Here, Oswald," I called, walking slowly down the street and looking up and down. Unfortunately, it was getting dark. Finding Oswald was going to be awfully difficult and I only hoped Norma would have better luck with the janitor.

But as I started down a second block, I saw a knot of people standing around a tall tree and squinting up at the branches. As I came closer, I suddenly heard a familiar voice calling down from the branches — "Avast there, you lubbers!"

"Oswald," I breathed thankfully. Charlie must be broadcasting into his microphone. Sometimes that boy isn't as dumb as I think!

"You know that kid up there?" a man standing nearby asked me. He blinked at my costume, but then went on. "He really can climb, can't he? Personally, I don't see how he did it. I can't even see him." The man waved at the tree trunk, which was long and smooth. The branches didn't start for fifteen feet or so.

"That's easy," I answered, without thinking. "He flew up." There was a series of gasps, and people started edging away from me.

"Maybe they both escaped from some sort of asylum," someone whispered. I felt myself blushing, but there wasn't time to explain. "Here Oswald," I called out in my sweetest voice. "Here are some nice peanuts for you."

"Avast there, you lubbers," answered Oswald — in Charlie's voice — from somewhere in the depths of the branches. "Avast there, avast there — "

"Well, there's no need to worry," a sweet-faced little woman announced, hurrying up to us. "I've just sent for the fire department. They'll have that poor frightened little boy down from the tree in no time at all."

"The fire department?" I asked in a sinking voice. Somehow, I didn't think the firemen were going to appreciate rescuing a bird from a tree. "You didn't have to do that, Madam. Oswald can get down by himself." And I waved my peanuts frantically at the tree top.

For a few seconds, the talking stopped, and I was feeling hopeful. But after a short pause Oswald suddenly started barking!

"That poor child. He's out of his mind with fear," the sweet-faced woman moaned.

"Nonsense, that's no child," a stout woman said briskly. "I know a basset hound when I hear one."

I do too, and something told me Barnaby had gotten hold of Charlie's microphone.

"Don't be an idiot, Mabel," a man said. "You know a basset hound can't climb trees."

The crowd around the tree was growing larger by the minute. Cars were stopping as they passed. And Oswald kept on barking! It seemed to me there was only one thing to do. I had to climb that tree and get Oswald down before we attracted the whole town. Fortunately, I had on my Indian moccasins and always heard that Indians were good climbers. So up I started.

I made it all the way up to the branches — and Oswald. The only trouble was I discovered that climbing *down* a tree was a lot harder than going up. The people on the ground seemed no larger than squirrels. With the key safe in my pocket and Oswald on my shoulder, happily chewing on a peanut, I clutched a heavy branch with all my might, closed my eyes and faced the dismal truth. I wasn't going to be able to get down from the tree by myself!

And then Charlie's voice sounded in my ears again. "For Pete's sake, Cass. What are you doing up in this tree?"

I opened my eyes, and there was Charlie himself, holding on to the same branch I was. "Unbarking Oswald," I sighed, and handed my redheaded cousin the small radio. "What are you doing here, Charlie?"

"When I saw the crowd, I figured they were probably looking up at Oswald, so I came over. Tell me, Cass, how do you think you're going to get down?"

"I'm not," I said shortly. "I'm going to build a nest and stay right here. But while I'm doing that would you please take the key and get Mrs. Stanpoole out of that closet?"

Charlie argued for a while, insisting that, with his help, there was no reason I couldn't get down the tree. But then we heard the fire sirens. Charlie decided it would be too embarrassing if anyone thought *he* needed rescuing. So, advising me to hold tight, he took the key and, agile as a monkey, clambered to the ground.

Gloomily, I watched his bright red head as he fought his way through the crowd and then disappeared. At least, I consoled myself, Mrs. Stanpoole would make it to the faculty dinner in time to be guest of honor. And I had Oswald for company — not to mention all the people staring up at me.

Then the fire truck arrived. Two firemen waved the onlookers back and set a ladder against the tree. The taller of the men climbed up.

But he didn't seem especially interested in me. "Okay," he said, looking up into the branches, "where's the dog?"

"There isn't any dog," I answered.

"Listen, Pocahontas, we've had about thirty phone calls telling us there's a dog trapped up in a tree. Those folks down below say you climbed up to rescue a dog. And if there's one thing I've always wanted to see, it's a dog who can climb a tall tree like this."

I looked him straight in the eyes. "I don't know what you're talking about. *I* came up to get my bird, Oswald."

The firemen squinted at Oswald, who still had four or five colored feathers clinging to his glossy black body. "You figured you had to rescue a bird from the tree, is that it? Afraid he'd fall, maybe? Well, come on, Pocahontas, let's get down. While we're chatting, half the town could go up in flames."

Down the tree we went, Oswald clinging happily

to my shoulder. I was so embarrassed that I marched straight through the cheering crowd.

But, of course, next morning the story was all over the *Courier*'s front page, along with a picture of me being helped down the ladder. It was so humiliating, I resolved never to leave the house again.

Five minutes later, however, Norma phoned, bubbling over with excitement. Because of the publicity, she shouted into the phone, everyone in town wanted to buy tickets to the play. We were completely sold out. And Mrs. Stanpoole was going to give five hundred dollars to the School Library Fund anyway.

While I was digesting Norma's good news, Charlie came over to the house. He also seemed about to burst with excitement. "Guess what, Cass!" he exclaimed, freckled face beaming, "Oswald is finally talking. He said his first word this morning."

"He did?" Eyes wide, I stared at the glossy black bird.

"Go on, Oswald," my cousin ordered. "Talk to Cassie."

The black crow tilted his sleek head and opened his yellow beak. I waited expectantly. "R-r-oo-ooof!" he barked.

Oh, well, as Charlie says, it's a start!

Charlie Goes to the Dogs

THROUGH the years, my cousin Charlie has gotten me into all sorts of trouble, but last month — *well!* In one of his bursts of inspiration, Charlie decided to enter Barnaby in the Crainville Dog Show. And the Crainville show is the fanciest one in our state!

"Charlie, you're not going to try to enter that lovable old dope in a dog show, are you?" I demanded.

"Why not, Cass?" Charlie asked, in a muffled voice. He was crawling under his porch. "He's a dog, isn't he? Besides, he's needed cheering up ever since he was chased by a squirrel last week."

"But, Charlie," I cried, "the Crainville Dog Show is for champions. They won't even let you enter."

"Oh, yes they will," Charlie said. He pulled himself out from under the porch. "Barnaby has a pedigree a full page long. Besides, I have a secret weapon."

"That means Barnaby is in real trouble," I sighed. Suddenly I felt something lick my ear. I looked around, and there was Barnaby, with his big feet, droopy ears, and sad eyes.

"Secret weapon or not, you'll be lucky if the judges don't take Barnaby's license away from him," I told Charlie. "Anyway, what were you doing under the porch?"

"Hunting for J.M., of course," Charlie muttered. "You haven't seen him, have you?"

I shook my head. "You're baby-sitting again, huh?" As usual, J.M. was allowed to play in Charlie's yard only when my cousin was in great need of money.

"I have to raise $25 for the entrance fee," Charlie explained. "But looking after J.M. is pure torture. Do you know in the past few days that little pest has gotten lost *seven* times? Somebody taught him how to play hide-and-seek."

From somewhere above us, a bloodcurdling shriek rang out. Startled, I spun around and looked up. There, in Charlie's apple tree, I could see a round object that was definitely not an apple. It was the head of John Mitchell.

"J.M., you stop that screaming and come down from there!" I ordered.

"Something bit me, Cassie!" J.M. howled at the top of his lungs. But he began backing slowly downward.

"Stop that racket, J.M." I broke in, pulling him to the ground. "Nothing could have bitten you."

"Yes, it could," he howled. "A great big black thing!"

"Must have been Oswald," Charlie said. "You probably wrecked his nest, J.M."

There was a sudden yell from the tree. There was Oswald, standing on one of the branches, glaring at J.M. Then he tilted his black head and opened his beak. "Rrroof!" he barked at us. Ever since his experience in the tree, Oswald has been barking like Barnaby.

"All right, Oswald, calm down," Charlie said soothingly. "J.M. is sorry." Then my cousin turned to me. "We can't upset Oswald now. He's my secret weapon."

For a second I thought I was hearing things. "That barking crow," I asked, "is going to help Barnaby win a blue ribbon?"

Charlie nodded, his blue eyes bright with satisfaction. "Watch!" he ordered. He beckoned to Oswald and pointed to Barnaby. With a flutter of wings, the black crow swooped down from the tree and landed on Barnaby's head. The big dog got to his feet and marched to the apple tree. He walked with his head high and a gleam in his eye, just like a champion!

"Why, he's a new dog!" I cried.

"That's because he's got a friend close by," Charlie explained. "Right on his head, in fact. It gives him the confidence he needs."

I could see that it was true. "But, Charlie," I said, "if Barnaby goes into the show ring with a bird on his head, don't you think the judges will notice it?"

"Details, just details," he assured me. "I'll figure out some way to disguise Oswald."

J.M.'s father agreed to drive us to Crainville, provided we took J.M. with us. Normally, Charlie and I would have shuddered with horror, but we figured that Barnaby needed all the rooters he could get.

Mr. Mitchell dropped us at the dog show at the edge of town, then drove off to visit his sister.

I looked around me. There was a big white tent and behind it were rows and rows of large steel cages. Almost all of them filled with dogs — all kinds of dogs.

We were in trouble right from the start. An important-looking man, wearing a judge's badge, suddenly loomed before us. "Here," he said sternly, looking at Oswald, "you'll have to get rid of that bird. No unauthorized pets are allowed here."

Charlie hesitated, but he knew an order when he heard one. "Yes, sir," he murmured.

When he came back from registering Barnaby and settling him in a cage, Charlie had figured out how to keep Oswald with us. He had a shiny straw lunch basket. In it were three ham sandwiches, a thermos of milk and one large crow.

"After we finish lunch," Charlie told me, "we'll fill the basket with flowers to hide Oswald. Then you can carry it right into the show ring with you."

"With *me!*" Horrified, I began backing away. "When did we decide *I* was going to show Barnaby?"

"Well, I can't carry a flower basket," Charlie said. "It would look silly. So it's up to you."

"Now just a minute!" But as we were arguing, I spotted the judge heading our way. Charlie saw him, too. He handed the basket to J.M. and whispered, "Quick, J.M., hide the basket before that judge gets here! Hurry up!"

The little boy was gone instantly, ducking behind

one of the cages. And then the judge was at our side. "Well, young man, did you get rid of that bird?" he asked.

"Yes, sir. I got someone to hold him for us," Charlie said. The judge nodded and went on his way. Charlie and I were about to heave a sigh of relief when it dawned on us that we had made a terrible mistake. Charlie had told J.M. to hide — and hide he did! We couldn't see him anywhere!

"Oh, Charlie, we'll never find him in this crowd!" I groaned.

"Don't get excited, Cass. We'll find him. We always have." But Charlie was looking a little pale. "Still, maybe it would be a good idea to split up — "

But at this instant, we caught a glimpse of a familiar figure, and I froze with absolute horror. It was J.M., all right, and he'd picked a dandy place to hide! He was in a cage with the biggest, meanest looking dog I'd ever seen!

"I think," I said in a small voice, "I'm going to faint."

"We haven't got time," Charlie told me. He dragged me over to the cage. Inside, J.M. was leaning against the dog's enormous side, calmly eating a sandwich. The dog was also eating one. It was all very peaceful until we opened the cage.

"Come out of there, J.M." Charlie said. The huge dog promptly swung his head in our direction and growled deep in his throat.

"He thinks he's guarding J.M.," I whispered to Charlie.

Unfortunately, Oswald also spotted us. Hopping to the handle of the straw basket, he gave out a friendly bark. The dog stared at him, howled and leaped straight for the bird.

He missed. While Charlie and I stood paralyzed, the black crow squawked in terror, and then shot like an arrow into the air. The dog started after him and J.M. hit him on the nose.

"You leave Oswald alone!" the little boy shouted indignantly. To our relief, the fierce-looking dog blinked and then obediently hung his head.

It was at that moment that the judge appeared again. "All right," he snapped, "I saw your bird fly out of that cage. Why did you put him in my dog's cage?"

"*Your* dog?" Dismayed, Charlie turned to the judge.

"Don't you know that a sensitive, pedigreed dog needs peace and quiet before a showing?" thundered the judge. And he began to give us a lecture on the importance of quiet.

"Charlie," I broke in, too upset to be polite, "the Juvenile Monster is gone again."

Charlie gulped and looked around him. There were more people than ever milling around, but there was no J.M.

And then Charlie pointed to the meadows. I could just make out a small figure moving across the green. "Come on, Cass, he must be chasing Oswald. We'd better get him before he reaches those trees."

"A juvenile monster?" muttered the judge. "Chasing your bird? See here, young man —"

But we were running again — about twice as fast as we ever ran before. Because the meadows were nearly ringed by woods that looked awfully big and dark.

Unfortunately, we just couldn't run fast enough. J.M. reached the woods before us. And once again he had disappeared.

"Oh, Charlie, what are we going to do?" I wailed.

"We'll find him," Charlie said. He stood very still. From somewhere in the deep woods, we could hear a faint barking.

"That's Oswald," Charlie said. "Chances are J.M. is with him. We'll just follow the barking."

Which we did. And about twenty minutes later, we finally caught up with the two of them. J.M. was fast asleep, but Oswald looked happy to see us.

Charlie heaved a great sigh of relief. "See, I told you it would be all right. Now, if we hurry, we can get back to the show in time to have Barnaby win his blue ribbon."

I sat down on a rock. "Hurry in which direction, Charlie?" I asked him politely.

He looked around us. Everywhere we could see, there were tall trees. "Well," Charlie said, in some surprise, "we all seem to be lost now."

"Just about as lost as we've ever been in our lives." All of a sudden, my voice began to tremble. "Charlie, these woods are enormous! What are we going to do?"

"The only thing we can do," he answered. "We'll stay right here until someone finds us."

"But suppose they don't?" I said. "We could starve here!"

"Don't be silly, Cass," he said. "J.M.'s father is a detective, isn't he? He'll know what to do. Besides, we can't starve." Charlie reached into his jacket pocket and pulled out a paper bag. "We've got dog biscuits here."

I just glared at him, but three hours later I was hungry enough to eat one of them. After all, I thought, they ought to be pretty nourishing.

"You know what really hurts?" Charlie said, glancing at his watch. "It's just about time for the judging. And I don't think Barnaby can win without us to cheer him on."

"Is that all you're worried about?" I demanded. "Charlie Harris, don't you care that we're hungry and cold and lost and it's getting dark?"

But just then, we heard a loud thrashing noise nearby and the unmistakable sound of an animal panting. It sounded like a large animal. Bears! A big brown animal came crashing out of the bushes.

"Great galloping galoshes!" Charlie yelped. "It's Barnaby!"

I opened my eyes. Sure enough, there was Barnaby.

"But how did Barnaby find us?" I gasped, jumping up.

"He found you because basset hounds happen to be members of the bloodhound family," a man's voice said. Mr. Mitchell stepped out into the little clearing and leaned back against a tree. He looked tired but happy. "And because he has a very good nose for a scent. How are you kids?"

"We're all fine, Mr. Mitchell," I assured him.

"Hi, Daddy." The noise and excitement had finally wakened J.M. "Are you playing hide-and-seek too?"

"For the first and last time," Mr. Mitchell said. And from the tone of his voice, I had a feeling J.M. wasn't going to do any hiding for a long time.

Anyway, it all turned out fine. Barnaby hadn't won any blue ribbon — he'd been too busy hunting for us. But the Crainville police department gave him a special hero's medal for finding us so quickly.

Next year, of course, Charlie is planning to enter Barnaby in the dog show again. But I'm not worried. Next year, both Barnaby and I are going to hide. Let Charlie try to find *us!*

Charlie and the Birds

I USED to think my cousin Charlie went looking for trouble, but now I know better. It's really the other way around. Take last month when Aunt Carol decided to give a very important dinner party for Uncle Ben's boss. Charlie *tried* not to spoil the party. In fact, he even left home. It didn't do him any good, though, because — but I'd better explain how it started.

Mom and I were baking Dutch apple cake — my very favorite food — when Charlie came clunking into the kitchen. He had a worried frown on his freckled face, and his red hair, which always needs cutting, hung down practically into his eyes. Droopy-jawed Barnaby came in too, and it was hard to tell which one looked sadder.

"Hi, Cass," Charlie muttered and then turned to Mom. "Aunt Kate," he asked plaintively, "is it okay if Barnaby and I spend the night here?"

I nearly choked on a piece of apple. Mom just sighed. Wiping floury hands on her red-checked apron, she asked, "Oh, honestly, Charlie, is your father punishing you again?"

"Well, not yet, he isn't," Charlie said darkly. For some reason, he was carrying an enormous chintz-covered bird cage, and now he set it down on the kitchen floor, and leaned against it. "I just don't want to take any chances. See, Mr. Avery — that's Dad's boss — is coming to dinner tonight with his wife and some other people. And Mr. Avery is kind of allergic to me."

"Maybe because you set fire to his favorite pipe," I suggested, brushing flour off my blue plaid skirt. That was what happened the last time Mr. Avery came to dinner, I knew.

Charlie gave me an injured look. "That was an accident, Cass, and you know it. And it sure wasn't my fault that the pipe was a collector's item and cost sixty dollars. Besides — " But Mom's cough reminded Charlie that he was getting off the subject. "Anyway," he went on, "Mr. Avery is coming to the house again tonight. There's an opening in the firm for a vice-president, and Dad thinks Mr. Avery will give it to him. At least, he'll give Dad the promotion if everything goes right."

"And you don't do anything silly and spoil the dinner party," I finished for him. Knowing Charlie, it was easy to see why he wanted to get as far away from his house tonight as he could. Even when he tried, Charlie couldn't help getting into trouble.

"Maybe you ought to visit Aunt Mabel instead, Charlie. She's clear out of the state."

As I was talking, Barnaby waddled over to me and licked my hand. I bent down to rub his long drooping ears and fed him some raisins. Then, straightening up, I turned to see what Mom would decide.

"Before I answer, Charlie, would you mind telling me what you have in that bird cage?" Mom's been nervous about Charlie's pets ever since he absent-mindedly left two baby alligators in the washing machine.

Charlie seemed surprised Mom would care. "Just a couple of homing pigeons, Aunt Kate, that's all. I brought them with me because they've got to be fed at a certain time each day. And Mom would probably forget on account of the party and all."

"Homing pigeons?" Mom blinked, and then her eyes, a lighter brown than mine, became very round. But I guess she decided that pigeons (which only Charlie would think to take with him on an overnight visit) were not as repulsive as some of his pets. "Well, all right, Charlie. I'll check with your folks and, if they agree, you can stay."

With a sigh of relief, Charlie picked up his cage. "Oh, they'll agree. And thanks, Aunt Kate, you've probably saved my life."

Whistling for Barnaby to follow, he headed upstairs. I was dying to see what the pigeons looked like, but I stayed behind for a few seconds.

"I'm glad you let Charlie stay, Mom. But there's one thing you've forgotten. It's Friday the 13th! With Charlie's talent for trouble, he'll probably send the whole house into orbit."

"Don't be superstitious, Cass." Mom smiled at me. "We've survived Charlie's visits before, and I'm sure we'll survive this one. Pigeons and all."

And, for the next three hours or so, it almost seemed as if we would. Charlie's homing pigeons turned out to be the cutest birds! In fact, I fell in love with the one called Princess, a small bird with spanking white feathers and the brightest black eyes you've ever seen. Charlie told me all about the way he'd trained the pigeons so they'd go straight back to his house no matter where they were released. Then, after supper — chicken salad, plenty of hot apple cake, and milk — Charlie even agreed to let me help feed the pigeons.

"I don't suppose you could train Princess to fly to *my* house, could you?" I asked wistfully, as I settled myself cross-legged on the floor. From there, I watched Princess poke her sleek white head out through the cage bars and coo softly at Charlie. He was taking his time filling the birds' watercup and Princess seemed to be saying "Hurry up."

"Maybe I could teach her to go to you," Charlie

said, thoughtfully. "Fact, that's not a bad idea. I've been working on a scheme to get a homing pigeon in every house. That way, we could practically do away with the post office. Let me tell you — "

"Charlie, it's Friday the 13th," I reminded him, hoping he'd get that scientific gleam out of his eyes. "Please don't work out any goofy schemes today."

"But it can't miss, Cass," Charlie protested, swinging around to argue the point, and — sure enough — managing to knock the cage to the floor. Instantly, all four pigeons were out and fluttering around the room, just out of Charlie's reach. I didn't blame them. Honestly, that boy *is* clumsy.

"Great galloping galoshes!" Charlie roared, making a wild leap at one of the brown birds and missing. "Don't just sit there, Cass!" he ordered, glaring at me, "Help me round them up. Quick!"

I didn't move. "What for?" I wanted to know, tilting my head back to watch Princess fly up to the ceiling light. "You said they needed exercise. Why not let them fly around awhile?"

"Because, dopey," Charlie snapped. But just then the birds swooped down toward Barnaby, who was resting on the bed. That big coward howled with alarm, leaped down, and galloped toward me for protection, so I didn't hear the rest of Charlie's sentence. The pigeons circled around Barnaby and me for a second. Then all four zoomed to the window. Charlie thundered after them but couldn't get to

them in time and the birds were soon soaring grace-
fully up into the sky.

"Come back here," Charlie howled, like a red-
haired Comanche. I was afraid he was going to leap
right out the window after them.

"Would you stop being so silly," I suggested,
pushing Barnaby's head out of my lap and jumping
to my feet. "They're not going to get lost. You said
yourself they're homing pigeons and so they're just
going to fly right back to your house and — ulp!"
All of a sudden, it hit me.

"That's right," Charlie groaned. "Those pigeons
will probably fly right through the dignified party
my folks are giving. Mr. Avery'll blow up, Dad won't
get his promotion, and I won't get any allowance 'til
I'm ready for college!" With a last despairing look
at the fast-disappearing birds, Charlie whirled and
raced to the door.

"Maybe your dad won't know the birds are
yours," I suggested hopefully, clattering down the
staircase after Charlie.

"Any time anything strange comes into my house,"
Charlie panted, "Dad just *knows* it belongs to me."
Then we were too busy running to do any more talking. Charlie's house is five blocks from mine, and we
got there in about five seconds. The only things
moving faster were the pigeons. None of them were
in sight.

"Probably flew straight into the basement," Charlie told me, as we circled the house. "That's where I keep them. Come on, Cass, here's the open window." Hunching down, Charlie scrambled through the window and I followed, keeping my fingers crossed that the grown-ups were safely upstairs in the dining room.

And apparently they still were. But not for long, I realized as I peered nervously about me. The basement was usually cluttered with Charlie's experiments, but today the long, dimly-lit room was bare and scrubbed-looking. Over in one corner, a round table had been set up and covered with an enormous gleaming white table cloth. And right smack in the center of the table was a crystal ball!

"What's that for?" I gasped, stopping short and almost forgetting why we were there.

Charlie gave me an exasperated look. "It's for the séance the folks are having after dinner. And that's any second now, so stop gawking and help me round up those pigeons."

"Yes, but — " Charlie wouldn't give me a chance to find out what a séance was, though. Practically dragging me to the far end of the basement — the part Aunt Carol uses as her laundry — he pointed out one of the pigeons sitting on the washing machine, and the chase was on.

It took us about ten hectic minutes to round up the three brownish pigeons. Princess, the beautiful white one, was still missing when we suddenly heard voices coming toward the basement door.

"Let's get out of here," I whispered, tugging at Charlie's arm. But he was staring at the round white table and didn't seem to hear me. I soon saw why. Standing in the center of the table, her white feathers almost invisible against the tablecloth, was Princess. She was pecking busily away at the crystal ball, too.

"Let's get her," Charlie said softly, and we tiptoed up to the table just as the door at the head of the basement stairs swung open. With one wild grab, Charlie snagged Princess, tucked her under his arm and we both slid under the table and hid beneath the cloth.

Almost instantly, we could hear laughter and talking all around us and chairs being scraped into place. Through the thick white cloth, though, all we could see were a lot of shadowy shapes. Well, I thought, trying to make myself comfortable on the cold stone floor, this is what usually happens when Charlie comes to visit. I ought to be used to it by now. Besides, it could be a lot worse. And that reminded me of something.

"Charlie," I whispered, leaning toward him in the shadowy darkness, "you never did tell me what a séance is."

"You'll find out in a minute," he whispered back, "and don't worry. My dad says it's all an act."

"Silence," a voice suddenly ordered very close to my head. I gulped, trying hard not to breathe. "I must have absolute silence," it went on, in a strange, hissing manner that made me shiver with alarm, "because my mind must be completely clear as I commune with the spirits of the other world."

"Spirits?" I breathed, and right then, I remembered what a séance is; it's a lot of people sitting around a table while one of them talks to ghosts. And, sometimes, I had once read, the ghosts actually appear and talk back! "I don't feel so good, Charlie," I told him, urgently, "let's take our chances with your father — "

"Silence!" the hissing voice ordered again fiercely, and I just froze into place. I mean, I couldn't even move an eyelash. What's more, everyone around the table seemed to have frozen, too, because there wasn't a sound from anywhere. There was the most complete, most awful silence for about half a minute I'd ever heard. And just when I was sure I couldn't bear it an instant more —

"Spirits, come," the voice called, so loudly that even Charlie was rattled. He dropped Princess. She fluttered away, bumping into the cloth, and Charlie flung himself at her, falling with a light thud.

"The-there's something under the table," I heard Aunt Carol say, in a shaking voice. "I felt something hit my leg."

"Nonsense," a man's voice said crossly. I recognized it as Mr. Avery, Uncle Ben's boss. "It's just your imagination, Mrs. Harris, unless Madame Claudine has an accomplice hidden under there. I'll just look and see."

"Oh, no," Charlie groaned, beside me. I buried my face in my hands, and wished I was a thousand miles away. But before the cloth could be yanked up there was a sudden piercing shriek.

"That basket," someone cried, "look at it! It's *rising* in the air!"

For a second, I thought I'd imagined it, or that the cloth had muffled the words somehow. After all a basket couldn't be rising unless Madame Claudine's spirits had dropped in for dinner. Unable to resist, I picked up a corner of the cloth and peeked out. And sure enough, a large straw basket was floating around in the air, at least two feet off the ground! With nerveless finger, I let the cloth drop. "G-g-ghosts," I chattered, while icicles dripped down my spine. "That woman called the ghosts and they came. Charlie, what are we going to do?"

But Charlie ignored me. He seemed to be more interested in the commotion going on in the room. Chairs were clattering, people were all talking at once, there were occasional cries, and the sound of things being thrown. "Ruined," Charlie muttered, shaking his head. "Mom's party ruined. And I tried so hard this time, didn't I, Cass?"

"What are you talking about?" I snapped, sitting

up in annoyance and, of course, cracking my head against the table. "Ouch! Well, anyway, it's not your fault that Madame Claudine can really get ghosts to come when she calls."

"That's what you think. Listen, Cass, there aren't any ghosts. The reason that basket is floating around the room — oh, great galloping galoshes, now what?"

A strange, unearthly howl suddenly echoed through the room, bouncing off the cement walls, and drowning out the loud talking around our table. An uneasy silence filled the basement for a few seconds. And then the howls began again — long, and perfectly horrible. I was sure I was going to faint this time. And, then, of course, I recognized the howls, and felt like an idiot. It was Barnaby. In our mad dash, we had forgotten the poor dog.

"It's a fiend," someone in the room suddenly moaned. To my surprise, I realized that it was Madame Claudine. "Mrs. Harris, your house is haunted. We must get away quickly, quickly. I believe it is after me."

"After you?" Aunt Carol asked. She sounded bewildered, since, of course, she must have also recognized Barnaby's howls. "Why on earth would spirits be after you?"

"Because," Madame Claudine whispered, "all these years I have been *pretending* to talk to them.

Now, they are angry, and for the first time, they have come to punish me."

"Pretending, huh?" Mr. Avery snapped, and his voice was hard and angry. "But you've been taking good money away from people, haven't you? Charging them fifty dollars to watch your silly act!"

But Barnaby began howling again, and the noise drowned Mr. Avery out for a few seconds. We could hear Madame Claudine all right though. Screaming something about wicked people who lived in haunted houses, she announced that she would not stay in this terrible place another instant, and that they could keep their money.

"Fine," Uncle Ben said, when Barnaby had shut up for a while. "And you're right, Madame. My house *is* haunted. Let me introduce you to our particular haunt." With that, the tablecloth was pulled up, and Uncle Ben's face was peering down at us. "I thought so," he exclaimed. "If Barnaby was howling at our door, I knew you'd have to be here somewhere. Although," he added, shaking his head sadly at the sight of me, "I'm surprised to see you hiding there too, Cass."

With as much dignity as I could muster, I crawled out from under the table and smoothed back my mussed hair. Charlie followed me.

"I can explain everything, Dad," Charlie began earnestly, his freckled face was smeared with dust,

and there was a cobweb attached to his red hair. Brushing it away, Charlie launched into a rapid-fire explanation that began with a pair of pet snakes that he had traded for some homing pigeons. He explained how we had chased the pigeons as they flew for home, and our scramble in the basement. "And then I put the three we'd caught under a laundry basket while Cass and I went after Princess, and that's why it was floating around, and then —"

"*Pigeons* under that basket," Madame Claudine interrupted, in her terrible voice. She had turned out to be a small, dumpy woman with a red turban wrapped around her head. Now, her dark eyes were snapping with anger. "Pigeons, and not spirits? I refuse to believe it."

"Funniest thing I ever heard of," Mr. Avery suddenly declared, and then he began whooping with laughter. All the other guests seemed to relax then too. And when they heard that Barnaby was a mournful basset hound and not a banshee, most of them began laughing too. Except for Madame Claudine, of course, who looked as if she would go up in smoke any second.

Charlie and I took advantage of the grown-ups' good humor by quietly gathering up our pigeons and going outside to console poor Barnaby.

So, actually, it wasn't a bad Friday the 13th after all. Mr. Avery was so pleased about the fifty dollars they were getting back that he was full of praises about Charlie. Uncle Ben discovered he'd probably get his promotion after all. Of course, Aunt Carol *did* say that Charlie would have to get rid of those four birds of his. But he isn't worried.

"After all," Charlie told me, with a gleam in his bright blue eyes, "It's pretty difficult to give away *homing* pigeons after they get to like you."

Charlie's Dinosaur

WHEN it's Science Fair time at school, I'm always tempted to leave town for a while. I mean, you'd be amazed at the kind of trouble my cousin Charlie can dream up in the name of science! But this year, I thought hopefully, it might be different. This year, Mr. Prewitt — our principal — had forbidden Charlie to enter an exhibit.

"Just because one measly model airplane got away from me," Charlie complained to me afterward, running a gloomy hand over his bright red hair. He had come over to borrow my history notes, and had then accepted my mother's invitation to stay for dinner. "It isn't fair, Cassie. Because this year, first prize for the best exhibit is fifty dollars. And I sure could use it."

"I'll say you could," I agreed. Charlie's one runaway model plane had done a lot of damage. It had flown in and out of classrooms for a solid hour, mostly through closed windows. "It's hard to believe one little plane could break six windows, though."

"Only five," Charlie said. "I don't have to pay for the one Mrs. Gravely broke when she threw her handbag at the plane and missed. Besides," he added, "anybody can made a mistake."

"But you make one every year, Charlie," I pointed out. "Every time you enter the Science Fair something awful happens. So, if you must know, I'm glad you won't be there this term."

"But I will be." Charlie helped himself to half of the jelly, banana, and peanut butter sandwich I was eating. "After Mr. Prewitt cooled down, he agreed that every student ought to be represented at the Fair. Even me. So he said I could help you with your exhibit."

"He *didn't!*" Hardly able to believe my ears, I gaped at my redheaded cousin. Then I let out a wail. Mr. Prewitt couldn't do this to my nice harmless little exhibit!

But apparently he had.

"Mr. Prewitt said your nature exhibit seemed to be the safest one at the Fair," Charlie went on, ignoring my anguish. "He said he didn't see how I could possibly get into trouble working with you on it."

"That's because he doesn't know you as well as I do, Charlie Harris. *Nothing* is safe when you work on it!"

But I was stuck and I knew it. Because, at first glance, my exhibit did seem pretty harmless. It was just a three-dimensional nature scene to be set up on a tabletop. There would be a painted canvas background, some trees and grass, a swamp, and several rocks. Of course, the scene was supposed to be set in the Mesozoic Era, a few hundred million years ago. In the center, there would have to be two or three clay dinosaurs. But how dangerous could toy dinosaurs be?

I calmed down and decided to make the best of things. And for a while, Charlie was surprisingly helpful. The very first day, he produced a rubber dinosaur that he'd seen in a toy store window. "When you blow it up, it's four feet tall," he told me happily, dropping it onto our work table. "That's why I got us only one. I want to have room for my pterodactyl."

"For your *what?*"

"My pterodactyl. You remember, Cass. That's a kind of bird they had in those days. Not really a bird, of course. More like a snake with wings, but — "

"A flying snake," I groaned. "Oh, yoicks!"

Charlie ignored that. "The only way we can possibly win a prize is to make our exhibit more exciting, Cass. And a fight between a dinosaur and a pterodactyl would be pretty exciting."

"Charlie," I said, getting nervous again, "Mr. Prewitt warned you not to get into any trouble. That means, no fighting."

Charlie blinked his bright blue eyes at me and looked hurt. "Cassie," he said gently, "this is a make-believe fight between a rubber dinosaur and a wood-and-cloth bird. What could be more harmless?"

No matter how I tried, I couldn't come up with an answer. Finally, I just sighed and gave up. Charlie could work on his silly flying snake. I would concentrate on making the scenery as authentic as possible and keeping my fingers crossed.

To my surprise, though, everything went along swimmingly. Charlie's pterodactyl turned out as big and ugly as I'd expected. It had nasty little eyes and wings that spread out like a kite. But at least it was authentic. I checked the one in our museum and it was just as ugly. And as for me, I painted a strange, stormy, lightning-streaked background that looked as if it might be millions of years old. It was all pretty impressive. But what was most impressive was that in the three weeks Charlie and I worked together, nothing at all peculiar happened.

"Charlie," I had to admit, the morning of the Fair as we were taking the bus to school, "Maybe I've misjudged you. You've worked like a champion this time." Last evening, Charlie had insisted on setting up most of the exhibit himself at school. Now, we just had a few finishing touches to do. "What's more," I added, "you haven't played a single trick. Charlie, I'm proud of you."

Charlie coughed. "Well," he said, not looking at me, "there are a few things I ought to tell you, Cassie."

A cold chill went through me. "What sort of things?"

Charlie shifted the large square cardboard carton on his knees and looked even more uncomfortable. "The pterodactyl turned out pretty big, you know," he reminded me. "So I figured that we needed a dinosaur at least twice its size. And it happened that Mr. Jonas had *another* rubber dinosaur in his toy store."

I was almost afraid to ask. "Bigger than the one we had?" Charlie nodded and hugged the square carton to him.

"How much bigger?" I demanded, getting more and more worried. I just didn't like the look on Charlie's freckled face. When he didn't answer, I couldn't stand it any longer and made a grab for the carton. It fell off Charlie's lap and a big glob of green folded-up rubber tumbled out and onto the aisle of the bus.

"Don't touch it, Cassie," Charlie ordered, grabbing my arm. "It's self-inflatable and you're liable to pull the plug and start the thing expanding."

He reached for the glob himself. But the jouncing bus made it roll. A lady several seats ahead of us picked it up for us. "Young man," she called back, "you should be more careful with — whatever it is.

Here — " But a button on her sleeve got caught in the blob's many folds. The lady tugged, there was an ominous *shooosh* and the mass of rubber began to balloon out. With a gasp, the lady dropped it onto the floor.

"Oh, now we've done it." Charlie groaned, while I sat paralyzed in my seat and watched our dinosaur grow. "I don't know how to stop the expanding gas. Hey, driver, you'd better stop the bus and let us out fast!"

"Next stop is two blocks down," the driver said, turning his head. Then he made a grab for his brakes. The blob was now clearly a dinosaur. It was already as tall as Charlie and looked as if it still had a long way to go. In fact, by the time the driver brought the bus to a stop and got the back door open, the dinosaur, its head touching the ceiling, was too wide to get through the door!

And it was still growing. "We'll all be smothered." I wailed, shrinking into my seat. Apparently, the other passengers had the same idea. After one horrified look at the growing green monster, those in the front began spilling out of the bus.

The driver was made of sterner stuff. He raced down the aisle to our aid. Several of the remaining passengers helped him get the emergency doors open. Then, with everyone tugging and pushing and straining, they managed to get the dinosaur out.

"And you two kids can get out, too," the driver

snapped. "No pets allowed on our buses and that includes dinosaurs!"

The bus pulled away. And there we were — Charlie, the dinosaur, and me — right in the center of Main Street traffic.

"Well, I hope you're satisfied, Cass," Charlie said disgustedly, leaning against the dinosaur's tail. "You've ruined our exhibit. We'll never get the dinosaur to school now. It's too heavy to move, and I doubt if we could get it through the doors — "

"Charlie," I broke in, trying to ignore the cars that kept slowing down as they passed so the drivers could gape at us, "tell me something. What made you do it? If Mr. Prewitt saw this monster at the Fair, he'd be furious. You know he expects us to have a simple little nature scene."

Charlie shrugged. "I didn't think Mr. Prewitt would notice our dinosaur. I mean," he added hastily, "I didn't expect it to grow quite this big." He squinted thoughtfully up at our towering friend. It was now about twelve feet tall and looking like pictures I'd seen of Tyrannosaurus Rex, the biggest dinosaur of them all. "Maybe Mr. Jonas gave us the wrong one. Anyway, I wouldn't want to try to unplug it, because I'm not sure what kind of gas is inside."

"Well, what are we going to do, then?" I demanded. "We can't stay here forever. We can't move this monster and we're already late for school. Charlie, what are we going to do?"

"I don't suppose," he asked wistfully, "we could sort of sneak away and leave Rex behind?"

I just glared at him. "There's a fine for littering the streets, you know. I don't know what they'd do to a dinosaur litterbug, but — "

"All right, it was just a thought." Charlie squinted at the dinosaur again, and glanced all around him. Then his blue eyes narrowed and took on that unholy gleam that meant he had an idea. Stepping away from the dinosaur, he waved vigorously at a passing truck and it slowed to a stop.

"Hey, mister," Charlie asked the driver, "would you give my dinosaur a push with your truck, please?"

"What's the matter, did he run out of gas?" the driver asked. But then he grinned and agreed that the middle of the road was no place for a dinosaur. Under Charlie's direction, he nudged Rex with his heavy truck over to the side of the street and right into a metered parking space.

"Thanks a lot," Charlie said. When the truck driver had gone on his way, Charlie dropped a dime into the parking meter and announced that we were safe now.

"But only for an hour," I pointed out glumly.

"It's better than nothing," Charlie said. Reaching

into his school bag, he pulled out one of our "Come to the Science Fair" posters and taped it onto Rex's side. Then he penciled on the sign, "Be back for Rex in an hour," and nodded to himself in satisfaction. "Now no one will wonder what a dinosaur is doing on Main Street," he told me. "Well, let's get on to school. I'll start the pterodactyl's motor, phone Mr. Jonas to find out how to un-expand Rex, and then — "

"Whoa, wait a minute." I held up my hand. "What's this about a motor? Since when does a flying snake have a motor?"

Charlie began to run. "Can't explain now, Cass," he called over his shoulder. "We're late for school."

"Charlie, you come back here!" I yelled. But Charlie always could run faster than I could, and now he put on a burst of speed that gave him a half block start on me. Even though I chased him so fast that hair streamed out straight behind me, I couldn't narrow the distance. And the minute he arrived at school, my sneaky cousin ducked into the side entrance and disappeared.

I knew he would be heading straight for the gym, though, to start his mysterious motor. With flushed cheeks and blazing eyes, I went after him, hoping there would be time to stop him.

But of course I was too late. By the time I got down to the gym, pushed my way past all the kids busy setting up their exhibits, and arrived at our corner, Charlie had the pterodactyl's motor started. The snake-bird's enormous three-foot wings were very slowly flapping up and down.

"Charlie Harris," I ordered, with as much authority as I could manage considering I was still out of breath, "you stop that bird this instant!"

"Don't be silly, Cass," Charlie said, stepping back so he could admire his ugly bird better. "We've already lost half of our exhibit. We can't have a bird who just *sits* there. After all, what's scientific about that?"

"Charlie," I moaned, wondering why I had ever thought my kooky cousin could change. "You *know* what's going to happen. That nasty-looking bird is going to take off, fly around the gym and knock over everybody's exhibit. And Mr. Prewitt will expel you for sure!"

"Can't happen," Charlie said and shook his red head emphatically. "I thought of all that and I made sure the bird can't take off. I nailed him right down to the table and I used enough nails to anchor a a blimp."

"Are you sure?" Suspiciously, I edged closer to the bird. Its feet *were* nailed to the wooden table. And it did look awfully real. Not only were its wings flapping up and down, but its head was turning slowly from side to side too. It looked almost alive, and for a second I was tempted to let it alone. But then common sense took over. "I don't care what you say, Charlie, it's too dangerous." Reaching for the key on the pterodactyl's leg, I gave it a firm yank. The key broke off in my hand and the wings began to flap faster and faster.

I let out a small scream, then clapped my hand over my mouth. Charlie gave me a disgusted look. "Boy, why they ever let you into a science fair is beyond me. Well, it doesn't matter. Soon as its engine runs out of gasoline, the wings will stop."

"Charlie," I whispered, clutching his arm for support, "Charlie, look out. The whole table is taking off!"

"Yoicks!" For a second, Charlie was as stunned as I was. The enormous snake-bird, looking more alive than ever, seemed determined to fly up to the ceiling. But Charlie had been right — it *was* anchored to the table. Now it was taking the table right along. Shuddering, I closed my eyes tight. I had a horrifying mental picture of Mr. Prewitt coming into the gym and seeing our whole exhibit flying over his head. Charlie and I would both be expelled.

But I couldn't keep my eyes closed forever. When I opened them, the table was back on the ground and Charlie was sitting on top of it, huddled next to the flapping pterodactyl.

"Don't just stand there, Cass," my cousin said with remarkable calm, "go out and get me a tiger skin, will you?"

"A tiger skin?" I stuttered, and leaned weakly against the table. Either I was getting deaf, I thought, or going out of my mind. "What do you want with a tiger skin at a time like this?"

"Well, if I have to sit here all day, I ought to look as if I belonged in the exhibit. And I *do* have to sit here all day, because if I get off the table — "

"I know," I sighed, "if you get off the table, it starts flying again. Okay, Charlie, I'll see what I can do."

There didn't seem any point in mentioning that there hadn't been any cavemen back in the Mesozoic Era.

From home, I managed to bring Charlie an old goatskin rug my father had bought in Mexico and a shaggy black wig I had in my theatrical makeup kit. While Charlie dressed in the boys, locker room, I took his place on the table. And let me tell you, those flapping wings raised quite a breeze.

When Charlie took his place again, he looked quite authentic, with his red hair hidden by the wig and the rest of him wrapped up in the rug. And when the Fair officially opened at eleven o'clock, Charlie and his flying snake were a real sensation.

"They both look almost alive," people kept murmuring as they filed past our exhibit. "Especially the bird!"

Even Mr. Prewitt was impressed. Of course, he recognized Charlie right away. "Only you would have thought of climbing into your own exhibit," he observed, with a sigh. "Still, it's a harmless idea.

Unless that thing takes off." Mr. Prewitt stared hard at the flapping pterodactyl, and seemed to be estimating its wingspread.

Hastily, I decided to change the subject. "The Science Fair is more successful this year than last, isn't it?" I asked, nodding at the crowds of visitors milling up and down the aisles.

Mr. Prewitt turned his attention to me. "Yes, we have had a surprisingly good turnout today, Cassie," he said. "A lot of our visitors say they learned of our Fair through an unusual publicity stunt. Seems someone left an enormous dinosaur on Main Street with our poster on it."

There was a stifled gasp from under the goatskin. I groaned too. We had forgotten all about Rex. Mr. Prewitt stared at Charlie and then at me. "The Mesozoic Era," he said, thoughtfully. "And who else in the school — "

But a huge policeman, walking down the aisle, interrupted him. "Mr. Prewitt?" the policeman called. "Are you responsible for that dinosaur on Main Street? Because it's overparked now."

"It is?" Mr. Prewitt looked at me, and I considered crawling up on to the table and hiding behind Charlie's goatskin. But then Mr. Prewitt smiled. "I suppose I am responsible for that overparked dinosaur, officer — in a round-about way."

"Well, I put in a dime for you, Mr. Prewitt, seeing it's for the school and all. But you'll have to keep that meter going the rest of the day," said the police-man.

"Oh, we will," Mr. Prewitt assured him. "Miss Cassie Quinn has just volunteered to feed dimes into that parking meter." He winked at me. "Haven't you, my dear?"

"Yes, sir," I agreed fervently. And that's what I did for the rest of the day. Around three in the after-noon, Charlie's snake-bird finally ran out of gasoline, and Charlie could get off the table and find out how to get our dinosaur back into its carton. Which he did. And, while we didn't win First Prize, we *did* win the prize for Most Original Exhibit, and Charlie managed to pay for the windows his plane had bro-ken. So we were more or less even.

There's just one thing that bothers me, though. "You and Charlie work so well together," Mr. Pre-witt said when the Science Fair was over, "that I think you two ought to collaborate every year."

Well, I don't know how you go about contradict-ing a principal, but I'm going to spend the whole year thinking of a way to do just that!

Shopping Spree

Wouldn't you know it — my cousin Charlie was picked to buy our wedding gift for Miss Evans!

"There goes the class treasury," I groaned, when Mari Ann broke the news to me. "Charlie will probably blow it on thirty pounds of monogrammed bubble gum." Pulling my sweater on, I yanked my long hair free and turned to face my best friend. "Honestly, Mari Ann, how could you and the other kids trust Charlie with all that money?"

"But, Cass," Mari Ann protested, "what else could we do? Charlie contributed a dollar to the gift fund along with everyone else. And his was the name we pulled out of the hat. We couldn't hurt his feelings."

"What about poor Miss Evans' feelings?" I wanted to know. Miss Evans is not only my favorite teacher of all time, but — imagine — she had invited the whole class to her wedding. Our gift to her ought to be something she'd treasure for years. Instead, she'd probably get — well, there was just no way of knowing what my kooky cousin could dream up this time. "Oh, if only I hadn't been out sick yesterday," I sighed, and shook my head. As usual, a lock of brown hair fell down into my eyes and I tossed it back absently.

"I think you're worrying about nothing, Cass," Mari Ann said soothingly. She reached down into the locker we shared, handed me my notebooks, and picked up her own. "Charlie may have been impossible last term, but he seems to like Miss Evans. He doesn't do *half* the wacky things in her class that he did in Miss Twombley's."

"No-o-o," I had to admit. Charlie was only kept after school two or three days a week this term. Still, every now and then, my cousin's weird sense of humor insisted on breaking out. And Miss Evans' wedding, I thought, with a shudder, was such a golden opportunity.

But then I had the solution. "Why don't we have a talk with Charlie?" I suggested enthusiastically, as Mari Ann slammed the locker door shut and we started down the corridor toward the exit. "Maybe Charlie would let us go along and help him choose a gift. Then we wouldn't have a thing to worry about."

I should have known better.

"Nothing doing," Charlie sputtered, when he finally came out of the building and we pounced on him. "I know my rights, Cass. I was picked fair and square to buy that gift, and I don't need your help."

"Yes, but Charlie," I protested, as sweetly as I could, trying to appeal to the better nature Mom assures me he's got buried somewhere, "don't you think a girl would know more about such things? After all, what do you know about weddings?"

"Not a thing," Charlie answered calmly, not looking a bit embarrassed about it. He seemed almost proud of the fact. "It so happens, though," he went on, "I do know what Miss Evans wants for a gift."

"You do?" Somehow, I didn't trust Charlie's grin or the glint in his blue eyes. They'd always spelled trouble in the past and I began to feel more and more uneasy. "How did you get to know so much about Miss Evans, Charlie?"

He shrugged. "Who else gets kept in school as often as I do? And every afternoon Mr. Jamison — he's the guy Miss Evans is marrying, you know — comes by and picks her up. When I'm being kept in, I get to hear them talking. So, that's why I'm the only one in class who knows just what to buy Miss Evans." Charlie paused, and ran his hand over his short, red hair. He looked at me expectantly, knowing I'd never be able to resist asking the obvious question. And, of course, he was right.

"All right, Charlie," I sighed, after an endless second or two, "tell us, what does Miss Evans want us to give her for a gift?"

Charlie's grin became so wide it practically dislocated his jaw. "You really want to know, Cass old girl? Well, why don't you come to the wedding and find out!" With that, Charlie gave a loud whoop of laughter, turned, and started running down the block.

Completely stunned, Mari Ann and I just stood there with our mouths open. Charlie was halfway to the corner before I could move. "Oh, that boy," I gritted, almost ready to weep with frustration. But that wouldn't have done any good so I grabbed Mari Ann's arm instead. "Come on. Let's follow him and find out what he's up to before it's too late."

"But Cass, maybe he does know what Miss Evans wants," Mari Ann panted, as I half-dragged her along. "If anyone would eavesdrop on a private conversation, Charlie would."

"I know it. But I haven't trusted him since he sent me a box of bath powder for my birthday. He mixed some gelatin into it, and I stepped into a tub full of jelly and — oh, my gosh!" I skidded to a stop as I saw a bus pull up to the corner and my redheaded cousin hop aboard.

Mari Ann and I just had time to recognize the bus; it was the one that stopped at Blakely's, the one big department store in town. Then the bus, with Charlie and our class treasury was swinging out into traffic and disappearing around the block.

"We'll never catch up with him now," Mari Ann gasped, her face pink from running. Leaning up against the bus sign, she tried to catch her breath.

"He may not even be going to Blakely's. Why don't we just forget the whole thing and hope for the best?"

But Mari Ann knew me better than that. I've never been one to just sit around, and this was certainly no time to start. "We're going to go right after Charlie and stop him," I told her firmly, pushing up the sleeves of my sweater. "No cousin of mine is going to wreck Miss Evans' wedding — not if I have to sit on him for the next two weeks!"

We caught the next bus and were downtown in less than a half hour. But then our troubles really began. Finding someone in a crowded department store like Blakely's isn't easy. Mari Ann and I went up and down escalators till we were both ready to drop with exhaustion. We tried all the places where a sensible gift-buyer might be — the linen department, the silverware department. That was our big mistake, of course. Whoever accused my cousin Charlie of being sensible? When we finally did spot him he was coming out of the Pet Department!

"I don't believe it," Mari Ann breathed, turning almost white. Then she rallied. "Maybe he's buying something for your aunt?"

"Aunt Carol doesn't like animals — except Barnaby," I murmured, unable to take my eyes away from the black satchel Charlie was carrying. I couldn't be sure, but I was afraid it had air holes in it.

"Charlie Harris," I called out, in a loud, angry voice, and my redheaded cousin, along with half a dozen other shoppers, turned around. When he saw who had called, his freckled face twisted into a scowl.

"What's the big idea of you two trailing me?" he demanded, looking almost as indignant as I felt. "Are you afraid I'll run away with the class money?"

"Oh, don't be silly, Charlie." Mari Ann and I went over to where he was standing, next to the glove counter. "We just want to know what you have in that satchel, that's all."

"Boy, are you ever a nosy female," Charlie muttered, still scowling at me. "Well, cousin or no cousin, you can just wait for the wedding like everyone else!"

"You mean it is a wedding gift?" Weakly, I leaned against the nearest counter and stared at him. Despite all the things I'd said to Mari Ann, I could hardly believe it. Deep down, I'd been sure that not even Charlie would try a practical joke on Miss Evans at her very own wedding. Well, I'd been wrong, and I could feel the hot blood rushing to my cheeks. Maybe Charlie had inherited Grandpa Mason's bright red hair, but I had inherited Grandpa's blazing temper.

"You hand that satchel over, Charlie," I ordered in a shaking voice. "Whatever it is, it's going right back to the Pet Department!"

Charlie shook his head and backed up so I made a grab for the satchel. It broke open, spilling a small black and white animal to the ground.

"Look out!" Mari Ann warned, as I automatically stooped to make sure the animal hadn't been hurt. He hadn't been, but when I got a good look at him, I nearly fainted.

"It's a skunk!" I breathed, almost paralyzed with shock. Mari Ann moved away from us, but I was frozen to the spot. The skunk didn't budge either. He just tilted his head and stared at me with reproachful black eyes. He seemed to be asking, "Why did you knock me to the floor?"

"So it's a skunk," Charlie said, as I slowly began to straighten up. "You don't have to act like that, Cass. He's been deodorized. Besides, Miss Evans *wants* one. I heard her myself."

This outrageous remark broke the spell I was in. Forgetting the skunk, I whirled to face my cousin. "You heard Miss Evans — oh, Charlie Harris, now I know you're lying. Nobody, but nobody, wants a skunk unless it's a mother skunk!"

"Is that so?" Charlie put his fists on his hips. "Well, if nobody wants them, how come Blakely's is selling them? You think the owner of this store is slaphappy or something?"

"No, but I know who is," I started to say. Mari Ann interrupted the argument, however, by crying that the skunk was running away.

"There he goes," she gasped, and I looked around just in time to see the black animal, his fluffy tail waving, scurry down the aisle and around a counter.

"Hey, come back here," Charlie yelped. Kicking the satchel out of the way, he took off after the skunk, his jacket billowing out behind him.

"Good riddance," I muttered, still feeling shaky, and smoothed back my hair. But then it suddenly dawned on me — that wan't just a skunk disappearing into the crowd. "That's our class treasury," I gasped. "It can't get away!"

Mari Ann blinked. Then, her face turned pale. "Oh, Cass, suppose Charlie can't catch it?"

"If he can't, we will," I assured her, already on my way down the aisle. And as I ran I wondered, for the hundredth time, how does Charlie manage to get mixed up in such crazy situations?

I mean, I'd like to forget that mad chase, but I'm afraid I never will. At first, the customers we passed thought we were after a black cat or something, and they just smiled and got out of our way. But, after a minute or two, people began to realize just what sort of animal we were chasing. Someone in the crowd hollered out, "There's a skunk loose!" and I never saw such wild running and jumping in my life. One plump, gray-haired lady climbed right onto the lingerie counter.

We finally caught our skunk, though. The little dope ran into an open elevator. Everybody else in the elevator, including the operator, came racing out. So we all piled in and surrounded the skunk; Charlie, Mari Ann, me, and also, I noticed as Charlie reached down and scooped up the animal, a big husky man with a very red face.

"All right," the red-faced man snarled at us. "You kids have just about turned this floor upside down, and you'd better have a good explanation."

I was too out of breath to talk and Mari Ann just blinked and looked as if she were about to burst into tears. Charlie, however, answered for all of us.

"We've got a good explanation," he said calmly, stroking the skunk's small black head. "We were trying to catch Miss Evans' wedding gift."

"That is a wedding gift?" the man asked in a strangled sort of voice. His face got even redder and I had a feeling he didn't believe Charlie. It turned out I was right. We were all herded down to his office for what he said would be further questioning.

There, even though we told our story four or five times each, the man — Mr. Kelly, who was, of course, the store detective — still refused to believe us. "I think you're working with a gang of shoplifters," he growled at us. "You three create a disturbance and while I'm trying to catch you, your friends steal everything in sight. That's what happened at Finley's only last week and — " He stopped, because Mari Ann finally did burst into tears and I guess I had a funny look on my face too. It's a terrifying feeling to see prison doors practically open up before you and I had to close my eyes tight for a second.

"Okay, okay," Mr. Kelly muttered, and I opened my eyes to see him hand Mari Ann an enormous blue handkerchief. "I could be wrong. Maybe you all were just chasing a wedding gift. I'll telephone that teacher of yours and see what she says."

"Hey, you can't do that," Charlie protested. We all stared at him. "You'll spoil the surprise," he went on, bouncing up from his chair. As we continued to stare, though, he gave a sickly sort of smile and sat back again. The detective grunted, and grabbed for the telephone.

Well, we were lucky. Miss Evans was still at school and she hurried right down to the department store and identified us. "Certainly, they're all in my class, Mr. Kelly," she told the detective. "If they want to buy me a skunk as a wedding gift, I'm sure they have a good reason." Miss Evans turned and gave us all an encouraging smile. Obviously she was waiting to hear what that good reason might be.

"Charlie said you wanted one, Miss Evans," I blurted out, and than tried to squirm my way deeper into the leather armchair I was curled up on. "He gets these weird ideas sometimes, but you know he really means well, don't you? I mean — "

"But she does want one," Charlie broke in, indignantly. "Don't you remember, Miss Evans? Mr. Jamison was telling you about all the pets he has; a raccoon, a hamster, a red fox, a couple of snakes, a spider-tailed monkey — "

"And I said," Miss Evans chimed in, with a sudden smile, "that the only thing we didn't have was a pet skunk. Yes, of course I remember it very well now."

"Snakes?" Mari Ann murmured, and gulped hard, practically turning bright green before our eyes. I felt sort of green myself.

Miss Evans explained it, however. "My future husband is a naturalist, girls. He loves all kinds of animals, including skunks. He'll certainly approve of the class's gift." She paused and took a deep breath. "And so do I. It's a very, uh, thoughtful gift."

"It's different, too," I agreed, and I could hear Mari Ann stifle a giggle.

"Well," said Mr. Kelly, "I guess you kids aren't working with a gang of shoplifters after all. You can leave now, and don't forget to take that — that wedding present with you!" He grinned at Miss Evans.

"He's even got a name," Charlie told us all, with a broad, happy smile. "The skunk's name is Orange Blossom. How about that?"

Charlie looked so pleased that I felt ashamed of myself for having doubted him. In his own way, Charlie had done his best to give Miss Evans the perfect wedding gift.

And you know something? Orange Blossom turned out to be the hit of the wedding. Everyone agreed he was not only the cutest gift on the table, but the one least likely to be forgotten!

Charlie's Going-Away Gift

LET'S face it — any time my cousin Charlie is put on a committee, the committee is in trouble, right? So when our class elected Charlie *president* of the "Going-Away" Committee — well, I figured the rest of us would be lucky if we survived. And I made plans, then and there, to stay home on Senior Day.

"But you'll miss all the ceremonies," Mari Ann wailed, when I told her. We were in the Campus Shoppe, and Mari Ann was so upset she nearly spilled her Cherry Float. "And you'll miss seeing Mr. Jacobs get his going away gifts. You can't do that, Cassie!"

"Oh, yes I can," I repeated, stubbornly. I felt terrible about it, of course. Mr. Jacobs, who was retiring after 40 years of teaching music, was one of my favorite teachers. And I did want to see the expression on his face when he saw the gift from our class — the beautiful gold watch we'd picked out for him.

"If only you hadn't put Charlie in charge," I

sighed, shaking my head and sipping mournfully at my chocolate malt. "Don't you know how careless he is? How absentminded? Don't you remember that Charlie holds the all-time record for losing library cards — seven in one month?"

Mari Ann nodded. "I know, Cass, and I'm worried too. But somebody had to guard the watch. With all that's been going on, lately — "

Mari Ann didn't have to finish the sentence. I knew what she meant. In the past few months, we'd had an awful lot of burglaries at school. Someone had been breaking into lockers, desks, closets — even the safe in Mr. Prewitt's office! Obviously, until the thief was caught, Mr. Jacob's watch couldn't be left in school. But giving it to *Charlie* for safekeeping? "That's like asking a *monkey* to guard your *banana* for you," I snorted.

But for once, it looked as if I were wrong. Charlie, who was just as fond of Mr. Jacobs as the rest of us, really seemed to be trying to protect that gold watch. He even remembered to deliver it to the jewelry store to get it engraved. Right up until the day before the going-away ceremonies, Mr. Jacob's watch seemed to be in good hands.

Even I had begun to relax. In fact, when the class elected me to present the watch to Mr. Jacobs, I was so proud and happy, I almost apologized to Charlie for the terrible things I'd been saying about him.

But then we had our dress rehearsal — and disaster struck!

You have to picture it. here we all were, sitting in the auditorium — everyone but Mr. Jacobs, of course, who was going to be surprised. At the very last minute, Charlie had come rushing in and had slipped me the small white box that held Mr. Jacob's watch. I was holding it tightly, afraid it might fall and break. Then gradually, we all began to settle down. It became very quiet and solemn as Mr. Prewitt slowly walked up onto the platform and turned to face us.

At that exact second, the white box on my lap began to blare out the Flying Saucers' latest hit record, *Green Mountain Blues!* Every eye in the auditorium — including Mr. Prewitt's — turned to me.

I was so stunned, I could hardly move. Then, with shaking hands, I opened the white box. Inside was a big gold pocket watch — and the pocket watch was *sending out music!*

"It can't be!" I thought dazedly. I looked up. Mr. Prewitt was still staring at me, in that icy way principals have when you've just done something awful. Clearly, he was waiting for me to do something about that terrible racket. But how, I wondered, how do you turn off a *pocket watch?*

Shaking the watch didn't help. Neither did sitting on it. And by now, a small army of teachers was heading my way with fire in their eyes.

I did the only sensible thing. Still clutching the musical watch, I got up, turned, and ran out of the auditorium so fast I bet I was only a blur. And right behind me, naturally, came my cousin Charlie.

"Listen, I'm sorry about this, Cass," Charlie assured me, when we were safely out in the hall. Taking the watch from me, he opened it up and somehow managed to turn it off. Then he ran his hand over his spiky red hair. "But I can explain the whole thing. Honest!"

"I'd like to hear that explanation too, Charles," Mr. Prewitt said sternly. He had followed us out of the auditorium and now stood staring down at us. I shuddered. From the expression on our principal's face, Charlie's explanation would have to be good.

"Well, you see, sir," Charlie said a few minutes later, when we found ourselves in Mr. Prewitt's office, "the jeweler hadn't finished engraving Mr. Jacob's watch. And I figured, since this was just a dress rehearsal, why not give Cassie my watch-reminder?"

There was a short pause while both Mr. Prewitt and I just gaped at Charlie.

"Your watch-reminder?" Mr. Prewitt finally managed to ask.

Charlie nodded. His blue eyes began to gleam, the way they do when he talks about one of his zany inventions. "See, I had this really great idea last month. I'm a little absentminded, you know, so I asked myself — why not invent a watch that can *remind me* to do things?"

Mr. Prewitt was looking more and more confused. "How," he asked in a kind of strangled voice, "can a watch remind you to do anything?"

"It's very simple. You put a tiny tape recording inside the watch — a recording that reminds you to pick up your clothes at the cleaners, for instance. And you set the watch for, say, four o'clock. Then at four o'clock — "

"Your watch tells you to go to the cleaners," I finished for him.

Charlie beamed. "Great idea, isn't it?"

Mr. Prewitt nodded, thoughtfully. "It is rather ingenious. But tell me, Charles — why was your, ah, watch-reminder playing that awful music?"

Charlie blushed to the roots of his red hair. "I put the wrong tape into the watch," he admitted, meekly.

"I see." Mr. Prewitt sighed, then told me I could leave while he discussed the matter further with Charlie. Thankfully, I ducked out as fast as I could.

Out in the hall, I found Mari Ann waiting for me.

"Did Mr. Prewitt suspend you?" she asked anxiously.

"I don't think so," I assured her, and I told her about Charlie's newest and most devastating invention.

"You were right, Cass," she agreed. "We should

never have trusted Charlie with Mr. Jacob's watch." Stopping short, she grabbed my arm. "But it's still *safe*, isn't it?"

I nodded. As far as I knew, Mr. Jacob's watch was still safely at the jeweler's getting engraved. Of course, Charlie would be picking it up after school. And a lot could happen before the ceremonies to-morrow.

"I won't let Charlie and that watch out of my sight," I vowed fervently. And I tried. Believe me, I tried. But my cousin Charlie can be awfully slippery when he wants to be. And for some reason, he seemed to be trying to avoid me. I couldn't catch up to him until the following afternoon.

"All right, Charlie," I greeted him, "where's the watch?"

"It's in my locker," Charlie muttered, and suddenly pretended to be very busy untying some knots in his sneakers.

I stared at him, appalled. In his locker? When he knew we'd been warned not to leave anything valu-able in our lockers until the thief was caught. I could hardly believe it!

"Charlie Harris," I said, beginning to shake with anger, "you have done some terrible things in your lifetime. But this time — *you've gone too far!*"

Whirling about, I marched grimly down the hall to the staircase. First I would get the watch out of

Charlie's locker, I decided, clenching my fists. Then I would come back and really give that boy a piece of my mind.

From behind me, I could hear Charlie pounding after me. "Wait a minute, Cassie," he pleaded, slowed down by his sneakers, which seemed to have gotten knotted together. "I have to talk to you."

But I just ignored him, intent on getting to the locker before it was too late. Unfortunately, it already was. When I got there, Charlie's locker was wide open — and there was absolutely nothing inside!

I opened my mouth to let out a wail of dismay. But then I closed it fast. Out of the corner of my eye, I saw a man slipping out of the side door.

In a second, I was heading for the door. If I could just catch up with him! But suddenly Charlie appeared. He grabbed my arm.

"Let *go!*" I snapped, pulling free. "Someone's stolen Mr. Jacob's watch!" And I began running for the door. Charlie was right at my heels.

Then we were out on the side street. Far down the block, I caught a glimpse of our thief. I didn't recognize him, but he must have realized he'd been spotted, because he began to run. Taking a deep breath, I put on even more speed.

"Cassie," Charlie gasped, trying to catch up to me, "would you just *listen?*"

"I can't," I managed to tell him. "He'll get away!"

To my horror, the man suddenly hopped onto a bus. I was sure we'd lost him — *and* poor Mr. Jacob's beautiful watch. Fortunately, though, the bus driver decided to wait for us. A few seconds later, I clambered onto the bus, with Charlie right behind me.

"Quite a run you two had," the driver said, with a friendly grin.

I nodded, too breathless to answer. Charlie paid our fares and then steered me to some nearby seats. "Cass," Charlie said, between gasps, "are you out of your mind? You can't tackle a thief all by yourself!"

I blinked. Somehow, I hadn't thought about that. Maybe because I'd been too busy running. But now that Charlie mentioned it — I glanced down the bus to where the man was sitting. He was pretending he hadn't seen us and he looked bigger — and meaner.

"Charlie," I moaned suddenly realizing what an idiot I'd been, "what are we going to do? If he gets off we won't be able to stop him!"

"I know," Charlie agreed. "Fortunately for us, it's almost three o'clock."

Exasperated, I turned to glare at him. "What difference does that make? He can get off no matter *what* time it is."

And then it was three o'clock, and from somewhere in the back of the bus we could hear a sudden, loud — very ominous — ticking sound! Tick tock, tick tock, TICK TOCK! It grew louder and louder.

"What on earth is that?" people began to ask each other. Everyone in the bus, including the driver, was now squirming around. It didn't take long for us all to realize — the sound was coming from that man!

And then the ticking grew fainter, and now a strange high-pitched voice called out, "Arrest me. I've just stolen Mr. Jacobs' watch!"

That voice came from the man's pocket! He turned crimson, while around him people began to giggle nervously. Muttering to himself, the driver braked his heavy bus to a stop.

"All right," the driver snarled, "what's going on around here?"

"Arrest me," the high-pitched voice said again, "I've just stolen Mr. Jacobs' gold watch!"

"You did, did you?" the driver said, marching down the bus to the man. "Well, why tell us about it?"

"I didn't say anything," the man muttered in his own voice this time. Getting to his feet, he tried to get past the bulky driver. "Must have been somebody else."

But once again the high-pitched voice demanded to be arrested. And this time Charlie managed to say that Mr. Jacobs' watch had indeed been stolen. "Maybe that man's conscience hurts and that's why he's confessing," he suggested.

"I didn't say a word," the man howled. He looked almost ready to cry.

"Yes, you did, young man," an elderly lady assured him. "The boy is right. It must have been your conscience."

"I don't care *what* it is," the bus driver said. "I don't like practical jokes — not on *my* bus. So if you want to be arrested, there's a police station on the next block, buster, and that's where we're going!"

Charlie and I, of course, trailed right after them. And when we arrived at the station, Charlie explained that this might be the person who'd probably been stealing money and valuables from our school for the past few months.

"Mr. Prewitt, our principal, figured the thief had heard about the gold watch," Charlie told the desk sergeant, "so he asked me to set a trap."

"What sort of trap?" the sergeant asked.

Charlie explained about the watch-reminder he'd invented — which fascinated everybody, including the bus driver. Then he explained that he'd left the watch-reminder in his locker, hoping the thief would take it.

"Three o'clock is just before the kids come back to their lockers. The halls are empty then. The police figured that was when most of the thefts took place," Charlie went on. "Mr. Prewitt was going to have a detective standing by to pick up the man who *seemed* to be confessing."

"A detective?" I asked in a small voice. "Waiting at school?"

Charlie turned and glared at me. "That's what I was trying to tell you," he snapped. "If you hadn't chased this guy out of the building, everything would have gone like — like clockwork!"

I just sighed, remembering the wild chase I'd had and how scared I'd been on the bus. And to think — for once in his life, Charlie had done something right, and *I* had come along and spoiled it!

Oh, well! At least, we had caught the thief. And Mr. Jacobs finally got his gold watch — the *real* one, this time, guaranteed not to burst into music or to confess to any crimes.

"Beautiful, beautiful," Mr. Jacobs kept saying. "Something I've always wanted."

There was just one little problem. Charlie was so moved by the going-away ceremonies that he decided to forgive me. And to prove it, he promised me a watch-reminder of my very own for my next birthday.

I have a feeling next year is going to be an absolute disaster!